Large Print Ada
Adamson, Lydia.
A cat named Brat

W9-CAB-860

A CAT
NAMED BRAT

*Also by Lydia Adamson
in Large Print:*

2 A Cat of a Different Color
8 A Cat in Wolf's Clothing
1 A Cat With a Fiddle
6 A Cat on the Cutting Edge
13 A Cat Under the Mistletoe
14 A Cat on a Beach Blanket
15 A Cat on Jingle Bell Rock
19 A Cat of One's Own
A Cat with the Blues
Dr. Nightingale Races the Outlaw Colt
Dr. Nightingale Seeks Greener Pastures
Dr. Nightingale Traps the Missing Lynx

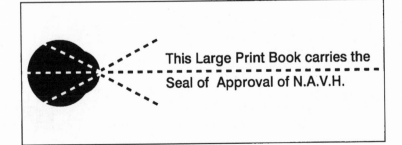

This Large Print Book carries the
Seal of Approval of N.A.V.H.

A CAT NAMED BRAT

AN ALICE NESTLETON MYSTERY

LYDIA ADAMSON

Thorndike Press • Waterville, Maine

Published in 2003 by arrangement with NAL Signet, a member of Penguin Putnam Inc.

Thorndike Press Large Print Mystery Series.

The tree indicium is a trademark of Thorndike Press.

The text of this Large Print edition is unabridged. Other aspects of the book may vary from the original edition.

Set in 16 pt. Plantin by Al Chase.

Printed in the United States on permanent paper.

Library of Congress Cataloging-in-Publication Data
Adamson, Lydia.
    A cat named Brat : an Alice Nestleton mystery / Lydia Adamson.
        p. cm.
    ISBN 0-7862-4757-6 (lg. print : hc : alk. paper)
    1. Nestleton, Alice (Fictitious character) — Fiction.
2. Women detectives — New York (State) — New York — Fiction.   3. Pet sitting — Fiction.   4. New York (N.Y.) — Fiction.   5. Cats — Fiction.   6. Large type books.   I. Title.
PS3551.D3954 C39 2003
    813'.54—dc21   2002073227

A CAT
NAMED BRAT

CHAPTER 1

How hot was that August night? So hot that even with both loft ceiling fans going at high speed and all my large windows wide open I had to abandon my bed and seek cooler space on the floor, using a terrycloth towel as a sleeping mat.

I was, by then, totally naked. And this, for some reason, unnerved Pancho a bit; he ceased his all-weather pursuit of nonexistent enemies. In fact, my stubby-tailed, dim-witted gray cat just stared at me as if I were a total stranger. Bushy, my Maine coon cat, would have been more sophisticated. But he was staying overnight at the vet, getting his nails done, his health examined, and his attitude adjusted.

It had been so far a slow, constricting, jobless, loveless summer. And it was not over yet. Most of my friends had vanished. Nora was once again taking her vacation on Martha's Vineyard. Tony Basillio was in Los Angeles, looking, he said, for work. Chuckle, chuckle. A. G. Roth, believe it or not, had gone to England for his long-awaited opportunity to make, as he put it, on-the-scene, hard-hitting inquiries concerning the British Secret Service's role in the assassination of Abraham Lincoln. His obsession with this case seemed not only to be ballooning, but now was a full-blown psychosis that in my opinion required hospitalization. I have heard that lawyers are particularly prone to this sort of thing.

The only one of my "circle" not away from the city was Sam Tully, but he was incommunicado unless you met him in a bar. And that I refused to do in the summer. In hot weather any type of alcohol makes me sick. I can't even stand to be around the stuff. Of course in fall and winter, and even spring, I'm a bit more tolerant.

I had been reading a lot, particularly Henry James. I had always disliked his novels and could never finish a single one. But I had recently found at the Strand a collection of his tales, and they were mesmerizing. Perhaps it was the heat. Anyway, while waiting or looking for jobs, either cat related or theater related, I would read Henry James in spurts.

So that is the way my summer was going — a little of this and a little of that.

That is, until the phone call on that hot night while I was lying nude on the floor.

Usually, when one is naked on the floor at eleven o'clock on a very hot and sultry summer evening, one expects some kind of romantic thing.

The voice, however, was very prosaic. So was our conversation.

"Is this Alice Nestleton?"

"Yes. Who is this?"

"You don't know me. My name is Louis Montag. I need a cat-sitter, and you were recommended to me."

"By whom?"

"By a man in a bar. I think his name was Samuel."

Uh-oh, I thought. If this Montag was drinking in the same bar that Sam was, it had to be a seedy, ugly bar. Did I really want to have a business arrangement with him? Any kind of arrangement? But he did sound rather normal.

He waited for me to say something. I didn't say anything. So he went on.

"Here's the deal. I need a cat-sitter a couple of nights a week. Maybe three. A few hours each of those nights, maybe between eight and midnight. The cat's name is Brat. He's not a problem, except he keeps bothering me when I'm working on my laptop. I'm a writer. He seems to be infatuated with the laptop screen. When I lock him in another room, he starts screeching. So that's what I need a cat-sitter for. You get it? I'll be at my laptop making a living, and Brat will be entertained by you, hopefully, in another room."

"Where is your place?"

"I have a loft on the Bowery. Just south of Houston. I thought ten dollars an hour would be fair. And an extra ten for the cab home. That would come to fifty dollars for the evening. Is that acceptable to you, Miss Nestleton?"

Usually, I wouldn't consider it immediately acceptable. Just on general principle. But times were bad. "Are you air-conditioned, Mr. Montag?"

"To the hilt."

"We have a deal."

"Good. Tomorrow night?"

"Fine."

"By the way, I never used a cat-sitter before. Am I supposed to provide food for you?"

I laughed. "No, not really. A piece of fruit would be nice, though. And something cold to drink."

He gave me the address and said that I should not worry at all about Brat — except for his laptop fetish, he was a delightful creature. Of course I had heard such claims before.

And that was that with the phone call.

I tried to go to sleep. It was a bit difficult. I read some James, but my eyes hurt in the heat.

At a little past midnight, I heard the blessed sound of thunder approaching. Louder and louder. I switched off the ceiling fans. The storm hit. Sudden and furious. The heavens opened. Wind and water whipped through my large windows.

As quickly as the storm came, it left. And in its wake was silence and cool.

I drifted off into sleep.

Sometime close to dawn, I woke with an itch on my left leg. At least at first I though it was an itch. But then I realized it was a bug crawling from my knee down toward my toe.

I sat up and leaned forward to swat the intruder.

Then I saw to my horror that it was a baby mouse crawling down my leg. I mean a very tiny and very young baby mouse.

Now, intellectually, I love and admire all God's creatures. Rodents included.

But in the real world I had become deathly afraid of them, like the stereotypical dizzy blonde who screams and climbs up on a chair at the sight of a mouse. It happened very suddenly, about two years ago. I don't know why. Maybe some complex reaction to aging. What was really interesting about my newly formed mouse fear was that it only became severe when I was alone or lonely or feeling abandoned by humans.

Anyway, I gave out one of those stereotypical squeaks of horror . . . half moan, half scream, all embarrassing. It would be hard for anyone hearing such a performance to know that the performer, as a girl, had calmly eaten breakfast every morning in a Minnesota farmhouse with clearly visible field mice chattering on a nearby kitchen shelf, looking for sugar.

The baby mouse dashed off me; obviously it now realized I was not its mother. It scooted under the dining room table, where it just stopped and waited by one of the legs.

Crouched on the floor about five feet away from the baby mouse was old Pancho.

He was crouched real low, like a leopard in the grass. If he still had a tail, no doubt it would have been twitching, for his eyes were focused on the prey under the table.

Brave, noble, modest Pancho. He would protect my home and hearth. I winced, realizing I was about to witness the central ritual of the wild — a kill.

The baby mouse realized his or her situation. It remained absolutely still under the gaze of that ferocious stalker, Pancho.

Then the baby mouse made his move. Toward the closet, where there were enough holes around the perimeter to move a regiment of full-grown mice.

Now, I thought. It's going to happen now. I braced myself for the carnage.

Pancho didn't move. He just sat there and watched the little mouse disappear. I felt a sudden rage. I screamed at him: "You coward! You traitor! Why didn't you protect me? Why didn't you *do* something?"

When I realized how ridiculous I was being, I just sank back down onto the Turkish towel and watched the morning light emerge, on the verge of tears, but never getting there.

The next morning I retrieved Bushy from the vet and told him the whole shameful story, saying that his partner Pancho had exhibited extreme cowardice in the line of duty. Bushy did not appear to be surprised.

In the afternoon I went to the Film Forum and saw a 1970s comedy, *Welcome to Greenwich Village*. Then I went to an air-conditioned Starbuck's on Spring Street and read Henry James on and off while eating a chocolate chip muffin and drinking two iced coffees. (The refill was half price.)

At seven-thirty I walked the six or seven

blocks to the Bowery and rang the downstairs industrial-type bell of Louis Montag's dwelling.

I was buzzed in. I walked up a wide set of concrete stairs to the third landing. Montag was waiting for me at the open door.

"Did you have any trouble finding me?" he asked.

"Not at all," I replied.

He opened the door wide, allowing me to enter. I was struck immediately by his height — he towered over me — and his crookedness. His shoulders were extremely uneven and stooped, and his elbows looked as if they had been broken and reset. He was dark complexioned with longish hair for a man his age — he seemed about forty-five — and he was dressed like a SoHo painter, in sandals without socks, a ripped T-shirt, and carpenter jeans of great age and disrepair.

He didn't look at me when he spoke; his eyes seemed fixed about an inch to the right of my face.

The loft was quite nice; sparsely furnished, freshly painted, and heavily air-conditioned.

It was divided in two by a single set of sliding doors. One entered into the work area. From where I stood I could see the sleeping area through the doors. That was where, I supposed, I would be entertaining the cat. It looked large and comfortable.

In the work area, where I was standing, there were two long tables meeting each other at the corners. On them were two desk computers and a laptop, along with a printer, a fax machine, and a bewildering array of phone equipment which spilled over onto the floor.

One wall was essentially a bookcase.

And one wall had a hodgepodge collection of blown-up book covers, hung with abandon in no particular pattern. Some were framed and others were not.

They were obviously the covers for different editions of the same book. And when I got close enough to read the title — *New York by Night* — I realized why the name Montag had resonated in my head with a gentle tickle.

Montag and Fields were the authors of this rather famous guidebook to the New York cultural underworld, if one could call it that.

"Would you like a drink, Ms. Nestleton?" he asked. I liked his formality. He asked the question almost with a bow. And he had one of those pleasant New York accents — soft and gruff at the same time.

I could see the tray he had set up on the sink counter in the small kitchen. These lofts all had tiny, open wall kitchens, put in when the spaces were converted from industrial use.

"Not right now."

"Well, please sit down," he suggested.

There were several chairs in the work area. But they all seemed to be knockoffs of the old elementary school chairs, with large folding arms. I smiled at the lack of options and sat down. "I'd like to see Brat now."

He replied: "I'm afraid he's not here right now."

"What?"

"Oh, there's nothing to worry about. He'll be here in a short while. The walker has him."

"You have a cat-walker?" I asked incredulously.

"Yes. Brat needs to get out. He's hyperactive. Someone usually walks him from about four to six. Today the walker was a bit late."

"On a leash?" I asked. I was starting to get a bit suspicious. Was this man just eccentric, or dangerous?

"Oh, no. Brat is carried to the park on Forsythe Street in a carrier, then let loose in a fenced area."

"I see."

16

"But why don't we act as if he is here," Montag suggested. "Just go into the other room and make yourself comfortable until he gets back. And I'll start to work."

Why not? I thought. I got up and walked toward the open part of the sliding partition.

"By the way, Miss Nestleton, I'd appreciate it if as part of your responsibility you answer the phone and doorbells while you're here."

"Fine. Is there an extension?"

"Yes."

I walked inside. The air was even cooler in this part of the loft. And there was a large, very comfortable easy chair with a standing light right beside it. I sat down, luxuriating in the coolness, and began to read a James tale called "The Altar of the Day."

After the first page, I kicked off my shoes. My feet were still not visible for the simple fact that I was wearing my long Virginia Woolf summer dress — a dull white flax affair that made me look like a lissome, ghostly wraith of indeterminate age stalking the downtown streets.

Time passed. The cat did not return. I put the book down. I heard the man working. I began to get more and more anxious.

What if there was no cat? What if this

whole thing was a setup? A way to lure me there? Why? Rape? Murder? Who knew?

At nine o'clock I resolved to just walk out fast. And then the buzzer rang.

Montag called in: "That must be Brat. Could you get him?"

I was greatly relieved.

I walked to the door, fumbled with the latch for a bit, and then swung it open. I saw something yellow.

And then I felt a terrible pain on the side of my head.

And then — well, just blankness. I was no longer there.

Sometime later, I opened my eyes. I realized I was lying on the floor, half in and half out of the open doorway.

My vision was going in and out of focus. The front of my dress was soaked. I didn't know whether it was blood or spittle or vomit.

I couldn't see a cat.

However, I could see Mr. Montag. His hands were tied behind his back. A rope was embedded in his neck. He was swinging from a light fixture, back and forth, like a metronome. But then he faded to black.

CHAPTER 2

To be honest, when I came to again, or re-gained consciousness, or woke up — I really don't know what state I was in — I felt absolutely blissful.

It was a kind of heaven, everything soft white and calm. And when I saw Sam Tully's old derelict face, I started to laugh.

"What's so funny?" he asked.

That's when I realized I was in a bed and this was a hospital room.

"Do you like my new shirt?" Sam asked, preening a bit.

"Nice, Sam."

He groaned. "You see how painkillers make a person stupid? You know you hate this polka-dot horror. I bought it on Fourteenth Street for five bucks."

"Well," I replied, "it's better than your usual garb."

At that point in my growing consciousness I realized, first, that the right side of my face and head was wrapped in a bandage, and second, there was another man in the room.

He was tall and slender, about forty, with a shiny bald head. He was wearing one of those rayon summer suits, but holding the

19

jacket. He wore a light blue shirt and a black tie. He was dark and rather handsome and he introduced himself as a homicide detective — John R. Lorenzo.

When he saw that his presence had registered with me and that I was clear-headed, he walked to the right side of my bed, rather close, rocked a bit on his heels, and said, "Can you tell me, Miss Nestleton, what you were doing in the victim's loft?"

I told him to the best of my ability everything that had transpired. It was obvious to me by now that Sam was right, and that I was heavily sedated, because I found myself talking easily, almost effortlessly, but there was the sense of a slight panic that I could not keep up with my words, that they were racing ahead of my brain.

"It was a bed slat," he said, identifying the weapon that hit me. Then he asked me what I saw just before I lost consciousness.

"All I saw was something yellow when I opened the door," I said.

"Yellow what?"

"Just yellow."

"You mean a man dressed in a yellow slicker, Miss Nestleton?"

"No. Just a flash of yellow."

"And that's it?"

"That's it."

20

"Well," said Lorenzo, "we think two men were at the door when you answered. We think that after you were struck the men entered the loft, bound Mr. Montag, beat him, tortured him, perhaps to reveal some kind of secret . . . it appears to be something like that . . . and then . . . with his hands still bound, he was hung."

It was a grim recital.

"And the cat?" I asked.

"We have not been able to locate a cat."

"And the cat-walker? He told me his cat was in the park with a walker."

"No cat, Miss Nestleton. No cat-walker. So far."

I closed my eyes. There was some pain now. I could not really fathom the fact that I had been lying unconscious in that Bowery loft while only a few feet from me a man was being beaten and tortured, for God knows what reason, and then lynched — and I was just lying there. But I truly remembered nothing after I opened the door and saw that flash of yellow. There was only that tiny window of consciousness afterwards, when I saw the swinging body.

Then Detective Lorenzo assured me that he would be in touch and seemed to ease himself out of the room.

"I kind of like that guy," Sam Tully noted

21

after he had left. Sam was now sprawled over the room's only easy chair.

"You know," he said, "this is a holding room for emergency intake. Either you move up to a regular hospital room tomorrow or you go home."

"I would prefer to go home," I said.

"Well, you do what you want to do. I've been feeding your beasts."

"Thanks, Sam."

"I guess I just can't let you alone for a minute," he said. "Because boom . . . you get into trouble. You're a menace, honey."

"I suppose I am."

"And I'm the idiot who really got you into this mess."

"It's no one's fault, Sam."

"Hell it ain't. Why did I have to open my mouth in that bar? I was the one who suggested you when he told me he needed a cat-sitter."

"Why wouldn't you? You knew I needed work."

I napped then, and when I awoke I felt lousy. Sam was still there, drinking a cup of coffee.

He said, "You up? Good. You know, I been thinking. I get the distinct feeling that this cop, this Detective Lorenzo, doesn't believe you."

"About what?"

"About seeing only yellow when you opened the door. About not seeing a shape or a figure."

"Who cares what he believes?" I replied wearily.

"You remember what Harry Bondo said in *Only the Dead Wear Socks*?"

"No," I replied gently. But I really didn't care and didn't wish to know. Harry Bondo was one of Sam's fictional creations. A hard-boiled private eye that had appeared in three books before the series was dumped. *Only the Dead Wear Socks* was the first and best of the series.

"He said, 'You can lead a cop to water but you can't make him think.' "

"That's a stupid saying, Sam."

The old man glared at me and then burst out laughing. "You know, I think you're right, in retrospect."

"Sam, do you think I should notify Tony and A.G.? And Nora?"

"Definitely. You want me to make the calls?"

"No. Maybe it's best to wait a bit. Why bother them?"

"There's no rush, honey."

My stomach started doing flips. I thought

of ringing for the nurse, but the stomach trouble subsided as quickly as it came.

Sam caught my distress. "You want me to get something?"

"No, it's okay."

"Are you scared, Nestleton?"

"I was scared from the moment Montag told me the cat wasn't there."

"You mean you didn't believe there was a cat?"

"Not then . . . and you know, Sam, maybe not now."

"If there was no cat, there was no cat-walker. And that means nothing and no one is missing."

"Yes, Sam. It means there is only the dead man, his killers, and me."

CHAPTER 3

I went home that night. I stayed in bed for a day. Then I went to the hospital again and they put a smaller bandage on my head and gave me a lot more pills.

By the third day after the bed slat had smashed into my brain, I was more or less functioning. The doctor at the hospital said that if the blow had been struck by an object with a point, I would be dead.

Five days after the bed-slat collision, I received a call from Matthew Balaban, whom I had not heard from in twelve years or so.

Of course, being a theater person, he acted as if we had met for coffee a week ago.

Matthew and I once had a brief affair after meeting in an Off-Off Broadway production — an attempt to revive interest in Genet in the mid-1980s. The play was *The Maids*. When I say brief, I mean brief. Two afternoons in his apartment. It wasn't bad; it wasn't good. Then I heard he had left New York and gotten a job in an MFA program somewhere. And that was that.

Here is the conversation, if I remember it correctly:

"Damn, Alice, it's good to hear your voice

25

again. I can't get you out of my head."

"Where are you, Matthew?"

"Uptown, on Seventh. I'm staying at the Olympia Court. I came in to party a bit and to see a few shows, and I realized, hell, now that I'm here, is there anything better than a Nestleton performance? Where are you working now, Alice?"

"I'm not."

(Laughing.) "Well, that takes care of that. So we can party together, anyway."

"I think not, Matthew."

"You married now?"

"No."

"Just quieted down, huh?"

"Was I ever wild, Matthew?"

"A bit. And a hell of an actress. Something in the hopper, Alice?"

"I haven't worked in six months, Matthew. And the way it looks now, it'll be another six months before I even get a nibble."

"It's a funny world out there now, I hear."

And that was that. He said he'd call before he left. But he didn't, and I didn't expect him to, and I didn't care.

Anyway, the call depressed me and then my head began to hurt. So I took a couple of painkillers, and they knocked me out.

Early in the evening, about six-thirty, someone rang my apartment from the street. It had to be Sam or a derelict or some kind of pitchman. So I buzzed him or her in and stood at the top of the landing, so I'd have plenty of time to dash for safety if it turned out to be Jack the Ripper.

I was astonished to see Detective Lorenzo walking calmly up the stairs, admiring the old industrial walls. He stopped at the landing one flight below me. I stared down at him. "Hello," I said.

"Hello," he replied.

"Well, why don't you come in, Detective." I swung open the door.

"I'd prefer to stay outside," he replied. Then he walked toward me, stopped about a foot away, and handed me a photograph.

I stared at what looked like a graduation photo of a young, pretty woman with very short red hair and a nose like a button.

"Who is she?"

"You've never seen her before, Miss Nestleton?"

"Never."

"Her name is Ginger Petrie. Does that ring a bell?"

"No."

He took the photo back. "Well, we learned from Montag's writing partner that this Ginger Petrie was indeed Montag's cat-walker. And maybe a whole lot more.

Anyway, she's dead. Her body was found in that park at the foot of Houston Street and the East River. Her throat was cut. It appears she was murdered the same night as Montag. Probably by the same people. They probably killed her first and took the loft keys, then went to Montag's."

"And the cat?" I asked.

"Not found."

"And the carrier?"

"Negative also. In fact, Miss Nestleton, while it has been confirmed that Montag had a cat, no one in his building or on the street or in that park on Forsythe Street saw a young woman carrying a cat in a carrier that night."

"Very strange."

Then something peculiar happened. He stared at me in a kind of wicked way. And he said to me, "Are you sure you were in his apartment to cat-sit that night, Miss Nestleton?"

Infuriated by his implication, I turned, walked back into my loft, and slammed the door shut behind me.

But the thought did pop into my head. What was I doing there if the cat was not there — and would not be there that evening?

CHAPTER 4

After that visit from Detective John R. Lorenzo, things became very quiet, almost as if I had not come close to being decapitated, as if there had been no horrendous double murder in my vicinity.

Yes, things became very normal.

I received a card from Nora on Martha's Vineyard that she was having a fine old time.

I got a letter from A. G. Roth in England, in which he stated that he loved and missed me greatly, that his research was bearing fruit — but he was not sleeping well.

Tony Basillio called and delivered a demented monologue about his love-hate relationship with Los Angeles. When questioned about the company he was keeping, he had to leave quickly.

Sam kept calling me with variations on the new plot outline for his next Harry Bondo book. Of course, this was also a fantasy in the old derelict's head. No one was prepared to publish his books anymore. He had tried to humanize and soften his main character, Harry Bondo, but he had done it in such a stupid way that the potential publishers just shook their heads. So now he had gone back to the original tough-guy Harry, with no chance of ever being published. On and on his efforts went with no resolution.

That was what was happening with me in the ten days between the bed slat to the side of my head and that very strange phone call from Ray Fields, Montag's co-author of the famous *New York by Night*.

It was a Wednesday, I believe. There was only a small bandage left on my head and face. And a small scar, which was kind of wild looking . . . perhaps I could move into TV as a gun moll or a *Femme Nikita* assistant.

The call came in about five in the afternoon. It was getting cooler, I recall.

"Is this Alice Nestleton?" he asked.

"It is."

"I am Ray Fields."

"I'm afraid I don't know the name."

"I am the co-author of *New York by Night*."

"Well, that's interesting."

"It is important that we talk, Miss Nestleton."

"Isn't that what we're doing, Mr. Fields?"

"What I have to say can't be said with any clarity or depth on the phone. I would appreciate it very much if you would come to my apartment. I live on East Tenth Street between First and Second Avenues. It will take you only fifteen minutes to get here. I'd like you to come now. Right now, Miss Nestleton. I know this is very short notice, but believe me, it's important."

Of course I would go. I would go no matter what . . . I would go no matter what internal voices told me: "Alice, don't butt in. Alice, don't get involved with writers whose collaborators have just been tortured and lynched."

But I didn't get there until seven. I window-shopped along the way in all the lovely East Village boutiques. Ray Fields had one entire floor of a three-story gray stone building. The apartment was like a large box turned upside down. There were a great many paintings on the walls but no rugs and very little furniture except for leather hassocks, which were placed all over and which one could just plop down on. In fact they looked quite comfortable.

Ray Fields seemed to be older than Montag, and he was much shorter and burlier. His hair was combed straight back and he was clean shaven. He had a large, ugly purple birthmark on his forehead.

The moment I stepped inside, I saw that I

was not alone. Fields brought me over to his visitors, without apology, and without any flair whatsoever.

He introduced me to a young woman, maybe thirty, wearing a very simple but fashionable sheath dress. Her name was Noelle Lightner and she was the editor of *New York by Night.*

And then he introduced me to Alan Petrie, the younger brother of the murdered cat-walker Ginger Petrie.

This young man was almost a child. He had the same light hair as his dead sister, but his face was so aquiline that the bones seemed to be in pain. He was shy and said not a word to me upon meeting, but he did take my hand and squeeze it, as if trying to transmit that pain. He was wearing jeans and a white T-shirt, and around his neck was a small and unusually shaped silver cross.

Then Ray Fields led me to a red-leather hassock and sat me down. He served cold juice all around — apple cranberry.

Soon we were all seated. It was not a sewing circle, but it felt that way.

"We thank you very much for coming, Alice . . . I hope you don't mind me calling you Alice. And I think out of consideration for your time, I ought to get right to the point."

There was a murmur of assent from the young woman, Noelle. Alan Petrie said nothing, but he was staring at me.

I nodded. Getting to the point was fine with me.

"We know who you are, Alice."

What in heaven's name was this man talking about?

I smiled sweetly. "Well," I replied, "I am who I am. I'm an actress. I'm a cat-sitter. I'm a resident of the far West Village."

"Stop playing with us!" Ray Fields said sharply.

I stopped smiling. I didn't like his tone.

"Listen, I don't have the foggiest idea what you're talking about, Ray . . . if you don't mind my calling you Ray."

Noelle Lightner leaned forward and said, almost accusingly, "You're the Cat Woman."

And then Ray Fields reached into his pocket and pulled out a reproduction of that old newspaper clipping that I had grown to hate. It was an article in a neighborhood paper written when I lived in one of the less affluent fringes of Murray Hill. The article was about an Off Broadway actress named Alice Nestleton, who lived in the neighborhood with her two cats and had helped the police to solve a rather gruesome crime,

33

using her knowledge of felines and people who live with felines. The last line of the article identified me as the moral incarnation of the comic book Cat Woman. At the time I had found it rather goofy. Now I found it embarrassing.

"Okay," I said, "what's this about?"

Ray said: "Let me tell you. We know who you are. We know you have experience in . . . ah, how shall I put it? . . . criminal investigation. So we wish you to proceed with an inquiry into the death of our loved ones . . . and believe me, they were our loved ones. And we want you to do it because the police are not doing what they are supposed to do. It is as simple as that."

I replied: "I thought Detective Lorenzo seemed quite dedicated to catching the killers."

"When was the last time you spoke to Lorenzo?"

"A few days ago."

"I spoke to him yesterday. He thinks the whole thing was about robbery. Kill Ginger to get the keys to the loft. Torture Louis until he reveals where his money is. Then hang him. Sounds plausible, doesn't it? It isn't. What money? Louis Montag didn't have any money. There was no treasure of any kind in his loft. *New York by Night* isn't

Zagat's. Sure, we have a good distributor and it made money for the first three editions. But now it's on its way out. It doesn't make a dime anymore."

"Did you tell Detective Lorenzo what you're telling me now?"

"Yes. He considers me a naif. Look, we have all discussed it among ourselves, Alice. We ask you . . . we beg you . . . please, conduct a parallel investigation. We will help you in every way possible. This atrocity must be . . ." His voice trailed off pathetically.

I really didn't know how to respond.

"Remember," said Noelle, "there was almost a third corpse. You."

"I am aware of that."

A blanket of silence seemed to descend. We all sat there in repose. Only the young man, Alan, seemed to be agitated. He wasn't speaking, he was just drumming his fingers on his legs — right hand drumming on right leg, left hand drumming on left leg. But while agitated, he seemed incredibly angelic.

"Well," I finally said, smiling a bit grimly, "if I was to conduct what you people call a criminal investigation, I would do it in my own way."

"Yes! Yes!" ejaculated Ray Fields.

"I would concentrate on the area I know the police are ignoring."

"What's that?" asked Noelle.

"The cat."

They all stared at one another incredulously.

"The cat," I continued, "if it is still alive. And the carrier."

"But why?" Ray implored.

"Because it — they — are not to be found."

They all nodded, reluctantly.

"But there is a problem," I noted. "I really don't know if that cat exists. I was hired as a cat-sitter and I never saw a cat."

Alan Petrie spoke now, very softly, still drumming with his hands. "Oh, the cat exists. His name is Brat. He is an ugly old orange tabby. And my sister walked him every day. She took him to the park between Chrystie and Forsythe in his carrier."

The young man, I noticed, had longish hair and very small green eyes with flecks of white in them.

Anyway, the die, as they say, was cast.

CHAPTER 5

The morning after that strange meeting with the survivors group, if I may call them that, I met Sam Tully for a coffee in a little place on Sixth Avenue.

"That scar looks good, honey. It gives you a kind of Dietrich panache. Like you're foreign and dangerous and sexy."

I told him exactly what had transpired in Ray Fields's apartment.

He listened quietly and then was silent for a few moments, putting his ugly, grizzled, endearing old face into his hands as if he were weary.

Then all he said was, "I don't think so, Nestleton."

"Don't think what, Sam?"

"That focusing on the cat means a damn. Look, that girl was killed in a different place from where she was supposed to be, right? She was supposed to be walking the cat in the park on Forsythe Street. She ended up in the park at the East River. At least ten blocks away. So what the hell does the cat mean? Maybe the killers flung the cat and the carrier into the river — sad but true. Or maybe they left the carrier at the scene, and someone picked it up and took the cat home. Maybe that girl never walked any cat. The whole thing sounds like a fairy tale."

"Sam, listen to me. There was a cat. And that girl walked it every day."

Sam started pouring buckets of sugar into his coffee and stirring it as if he was rowing. He began to light a cigarette, and I pointed out to him that the place was now nonsmoking. He dropped the cigarette onto the table.

"You want to listen carefully to what I got to say, honey?"

"Of course."

"Good. Now let's start at the beginning. How did you get into this mess? I'll tell you. I meet a guy in a bar . . . I don't know him from Adam . . . we get to talking . . . he tells me he needs a cat-sitter . . . I give him your name and number. Right?"

"Right."

"But there was something I didn't tell you, honey."

"What's that?"

"What the guy was doing in the bar before I started up this conversation with him. Or rather, before he started up the conversation with me — because as you well know, honey, I don't get friendly in strange bars, which is why I'm still alive.

38

He was arguing with the bartender."

"So?"

"So nothing and so everything."

"What were they arguing about?"

"I don't know, but it was getting nasty."

"Okay. I agree it might be something. What do you suggest I do?"

"I suggest we both go there and talk to that bartender."

"I'm game."

"The best time is about three in the afternoon. The place is on Fourteenth and Ninth. It's called Bass Line. Meet me in front of there about three. Okay?"

"Okay."

"Fine!" Then Sam said, "Wait. Let's make it around two-thirty. And let's make it at Fourteenth and Eighth, a block away from the Bass Line. And you buy that book, *New York by Night*. Let's take a look at it before we go in there. You got it? The northeast corner of Fourteenth and Eighth around two-thirty. And bring the book."

Sam was starting to sound as if Ray and his friends had asked *him* to conduct a criminal investigation. But that was Sam, always a tad too exuberant given his age and physical condition.

So ubiquitous was *New York by Night* that

I found it at the newspaper store. In fact it was the only guidebook sold there, and it was shelved with the road atlases and subway maps.

Sam was waiting for me, and that was when I realized he was going to take us into another bar to prepare us to go into the assigned bar of our investigation. I dutifully followed him into a pub on Eighth Avenue between 14th and 15th Streets.

He ordered a bourbon on the rocks; I ordered a tonic water. We sat together and studied the document: *New York by Night*, 12th edition, by Louis Montag and Ray Fields.

"First of all," said Sam, "let's see if Bass Line is in the book."

The book was arranged by borough and then by neighborhood and then alphabetically by name of establishment. There was a straight alpha index in the back.

Contained within were places in the five boroughs of New York City that served any combination of food, drink, and entertainment. Only drink was a necessity for inclusion.

There was a brief description (sometimes not so brief) of each establishment, interviews with the owners, bartenders, and patrons, and complete information on prices,

40

hours, and dress code.

The blurb on the back of the book said it had become "the definitive bar guide to New York." Well, maybe. But the Bass Line wasn't in it at all.

"Do you find that peculiar?" I asked Sam.

"No. There must be hundreds of bars that aren't listed. This guide really isn't about neighborhood bars. I figure it's for people visiting New York. Young people who live in the city don't need *New York by Night*. They got free papers like the *Press* and the *Voice* which always cover the hip new bars. And then there's *Time Out*. And there's even a new mag called *411*, which deals with bars exclusively."

Sam started leafing through the book, shaking his head, mumbling in affirmation or disgust.

Then he handed the book back to me. "Well, let me tell you, I am not going to say anything bad about this book. And you know why, honey? Because it is one of the few that profiles the jukebox in each bar. And that is very important. How many times in my young life have I been wandering about and located a treasure of a bar on some street, and I went in and I said to myself, 'This is home, this is the place I am looking for . . .' and then I went to the jukebox and *wham!* It was all over, baby. You know what I mean?"

"Of course, Sam. Shouldn't we head to the Bass Line?"

He finished his drink.

The Bass Line was quite nice. It was one of those transitional places that had shifted gears as the neighborhood itself had changed; formerly an ugly working man's pub in the meat market, it had recently transformed itself into a hip watering hole. Nothing had been done to the interior, but the counter behind the old bar now contained the signature exotic Scotches favored by a clientele with some money to spend.

As we walked in, Sam whispered in my ear, "In the sixties and seventies, this was a rathole."

There were only two customers in the bar. They were seated together drinking bottled beer. The air conditioning was ferocious in its delivery of cold air, but one heard only a slight hum. There was no music playing.

The bartender was fiddling with one of the taps. She was young and very pretty, with black hair pulled back into a ponytail. She was wearing a blouse tied into a knot at the bottom, exposing her stomach.

It was funny what happened next — to me, to my head — though it really has no

42

bearing on the case. But I think I should re-count it.

At the sight of the young bartender wearing her blouse that way, I was hit by a wave of sadness . . . a kind of creepy nostalgia . . . a kind of ridiculous self-pity at my aging.

When I was in high school, oh so long ago, we always used to wear our blouses like that, in the short, warm Minnesota spring. In those days I was so tall and willowy and blond, I looked like a generic girl named Sally, on her way to New York to do musical comedy.

Sam ordered a brandy and a cup of coffee. I ordered a ginger ale with a piece of lime. The drinks were served in pleasant manner.

Sam said, "What happened to the guy who used to work here?"

"I hear he quit," the girl said.

"Quit or fired?" Sam asked, pouring some brandy into the coffee.

Her voice turned steely. "I said 'quit', didn't I?" And then she calmed down and smiled. "Actually, I don't know. I just started working here. Believe what you want to believe. I don't know."

"You got me wrong, honey."

"Okay."

"We're not here to start any trouble for

the guy. It's a personal matter. Can you give me his name?"

She looked at Sam in a weary, exasperated manner and then looked at me. Was she going to tug the bow of her blouse?

She said, "I think his name is Ted Lary."

"Do you know where he lives?" Sam persisted. The old guy was like a bulldog.

"No."

"Can you find out for us?"

"No."

"Do you know what he's doing now?"

"No."

"You know where he worked before?"

"No."

"His telephone number?"

"No."

"Well, thank you, miss." He added under his breath, "Thanks for nothing."

Sam started mumbling to himself. I was still lost in the fog of blouse nostalgia.

Then he spoke to me directly: "Okay, Nestleton. Why don't you go ahead and look for that cat. I gotta think."

CHAPTER 6

The next meeting of the group, the crew, or whatever we were called by then, was in Noelle Lightner's office at the firm that published *New York by Night* — Hermes Press, located in the Flatiron Building.

I was there in my new capacity as leader of the group. I felt I was back at the New School teaching my course on "The New York Actress." Of course, I should have felt I was leading a criminal task force.

That day I had a splitting headache, which kept appearing and vanishing, a result of the fact that the physical was finally weaning me from the painkiller.

The class was all there — Ray, Alan, and Noelle.

Noelle's office was large, like a storeroom, and products of the Hermes Press — guidebooks, road atlases, car repair manuals — were prominently displayed on the walls in the form of cover blowups.

Noelle had provided containers of coffee and miniature cheese, prune, and cherry danishes.

They waited for instructions from the Cat Woman. I felt for one instant like a total idiot. But then, ever the trouper, I began my lecture.

"Montag, as we know, lived on the Bowery, on the west side of the street, between Houston and Prince. Whatever shopping and socializing he did in the neighborhood had to be done on Prince, Elizabeth, and Mott. So, I think each of us should have responsibility for one of those streets. Agreed?"

They agreed and the streets were parceled out. Alan wanted Mott; Noelle volunteered for Elizabeth; Ray settled for Prince. That left the Bowery for me, which didn't bother me at all, since most of the Bowery down there was commercial restaurant supply stores with owners who probably didn't even know Montag and Brat existed.

"What do we do once we get there?" Noelle inquired pleasantly. She was seated behind a large metal desk piled high with page proofs of various projects. She seemed to be a stapler afficionado; there were four of them visible on the top of her desk, one of them obviously an industrial antique. Once again Noelle was dressed quite fashionably, given the circumstances, in a pale yellow dress. I realized she was a bit older than I had originally thought.

"There is no doubt that most of the

people you talk to" — at this point I was rather shocked by their rapt attention; they truly believed the Cat Woman was addressing them — "will already have been questioned by the police. They routinely canvass the neighborhood. But they were asking these kinds of questions: 'What do you know about Louis Montag? Did you see any suspicious people hanging around on the night of the murder?' Right? Now, we are going to ask a totally different kind of question and never bring up the name Louis Montag or Ginger Petrie until the person does. We are going to inquire about a lost or dead cat. Right? And believe me, you will be astonished at how people will open up when they think you're looking for a lost animal. They will tell you things they would not tell their shrinks, their lovers, or their priests.

"So you simply walk in with a photo of Brat and ask: 'Have you seen this cat? Do you know this cat? Have you ever seen a cat like this in a carrier with a young woman or a middle-aged man?' Understand? These are the kinds of things you ask."

I shut up then. I was beginning to sound like a self-help guru.

"Where do we get a picture of Brat?" Ray asked.

"I can draw him," Alan said. He was not

sitting, like the rest of us, but leaning casually against the wall. He kept looking at me and then away from me. His light hair looked even longer than the first time we'd met; it tumbled down his back in curls.

"We have a library here," Noelle said. "A very extensive one. There have to be some cat breed books."

"Worth a try," agreed Ray.

Noelle left the room and came back three minutes later, smiling and holding up a large-format book detailing and illustrating every breed of domestic cat throughout the world.

There were plenty of American shorthairs and one beautiful orange tabby shorthair in color. A female, but that didn't matter.

Noelle made four copies on the color copier and distributed them.

"What time is it now?" I asked.

Ray answered, "Almost noon."

"Fine. I suggest that we all get downtown about 3 p.m. Each one to his own street. And afterwards let's meet in that muffin place on Prince Street."

"I don't know it," said Noelle.

"On Prince, between Elizabeth and the Bowery. You can't miss it. Let's make the meeting at five. We each have two hours to make the inquiries."

There was general agreement on the plan. The conspirators disbanded.

Alan caught up with me on Fifth Avenue as I was walking downtown.

He called out my name and touched my arm, but then pulled away quickly, as if he had been scalded.

"You are very kind to help us like this," he noted softly.

I didn't answer. I was astonished once again by the young man's eyes and the re-markable shape of his face. He looked very tough and very vulnerable at the same time. We were standing close to each other, and I could hear myself breathe.

He pulled something out of his pocket and handed it to me. It was something wrapped in tissue.

"I got it for you in Chinatown," he said. "It's for luck."

I spread the tissue carefully. Lying in the center was a tiny jade pin. A cat in a position of anger and fear. Claws out, back arched, spitting.

"Beautiful," I whispered. He was smiling at me, almost purring. Alice, I thought, what is happening here?

Why was I in that muffin shop on Prince Street an hour early?

I had made only two stops, both of them restaurant supply houses, and showed my Brat likeness to uninterested Asians with a poor command of English. Needless to say, there was no recognition.

Sitting there, I was struck by the fact that I had probably orchestrated one of the stupidest posse hunts in recorded history. I began to feel profound embarrassment that they were wandering about the neighborhood under the Cat Woman's instructions.

I ordered an iced coffee and waited.

I tried to read a short story in my Henry James collection, but my eyes kept wandering out to the street. Prince Street was beautiful there — lined with narrow, old, pastel-colored houses.

And, as the hour approached five, the foot traffic increased. Asian men and women heading to Chinatown. Old Italian women visiting neighbors. Wealthy young lawyers heading to posh new bars. Tall, elegant models in mufti going who knows where. Derelicts heading for the last remaining soup kitchens on the Bowery. Tourists with their pocket guidebooks open. Shoppers peering into the new shabby-chic boutiques.

At four-fifty, Noelle Lightner entered.

The poor woman looked exhausted. She

sat down nest to me and let her crumpled Xerox of an orange tabby flutter down onto the tabletop.

"Nothing," she said. "Nothing at all."

I bought her an iced coffee.

"It's not that the people I spoke to weren't nice. They were. And concerned. But none of them had ever seen or known anything about such a cat."

We both sat there in silence and waited for the others. To say that the mood was despondent would be belaboring the obvious.

Five o'clock passed and then five-fifteen.

At about five-twenty-five Alan Petrie sauntered in. He saw us, waved as if we were casual acquaintances, purchased a chocolate chip muffin, took a large bite out of it, and then came to our table and stood there. I began to get uncomfortable.

When he finished the muffin, he sat down. And he started to talk, very fast indeed. Quiet and fast and excited, and anyone listening couldn't help being drawn in.

"On Mott, just before you get to Spring. On the west side of the street. There's a little ladies' hair-cutting shop. Not one of the new ones. An old one. They were very nice. They all looked at what I showed them and one of the ladies, she said, 'Oh, of course I know that cat. But I haven't seen it in a while. In a couple of years.' So then I asked her whose cat it was. And she said, 'Pia Jonas.' And then she said, 'If you don't know who owns the cat, why are you asking about it?' and I said, 'It's a voodoo cat.' And everyone laughed. And they told me that this Pia Jonas lives in the big gray building on the corner of Spring and Mott."

"What does it mean?" Noelle asked.

"It may mean nothing," I said. "It may just be a coincidence. It probably is. Orange tabby shorthairs are ubiquitous in the city."

"I like that word, ubiquitous," said Alan Petrie. But his face had suddenly become mournful. And this mournfulness seemed to suffuse the muffin shop completely. As if a blanket had dropped over it. He must have been thinking about his sister. I wanted to console him.

Then Ray Fields walked in. He was hot and disgusted and tired. He had found nothing.

Noelle told him what Alan had uncovered.

"What do we do?" was his astonished reply.

I decided it was time for me to get into character: full-blown Cat Woman. It was what they expected me to do, wasn't it?

★ ★ ★

I went to Pia Jonas alone, that same evening, above their protestations. I sent them home and promised to notify them immediately if the lead panned out. The idea of bringing Alan Petrie along was quite tempting; after all, he had discovered the information. But something kept telling me to stay away from this young man as much as possible. Stay away, Alice.

Pia Jonas lived in a fifth-floor apartment. The building's elevator was broken; it was a long way up a narrow, treacherous staircase. The scent of diffuse spices permeated the hallway. Italian spices, Chinese, Indian.

She had buzzed me in immediately when I shouted into the antiquated intercom that I was there to talk to her about an orange shorthair tabby — that the women in the hair-cutting place on Mott Street had given me her name.

She was waiting for me outside the door of her apartment when my climb was over.

I was immediately struck by her bizarre appearance. On second thought, not bizarre. Just out of place. She looked like a big farm lady beyond child-bearing years. Her shoulders were wide, her housedress worn, and her thick, ugly gray hair was fastened with pins and rubber bands. All her bones seem to jut out arthritically.

"Who are you? What do you want? What were you babbling about? What cat?" She fired the questions at me in a raucous voice, like a gym teacher talking to fractious girls.

"I'm sorry to intrude like this," I said, still breathing hard from the climb.

And then I flashed the feline photo Xerox.

She brought her hand to her mouth and stepped back so quickly that she banged her head against the door jamb.

Recovering from her shock, she asked, "Is that Bright?"

"What? Bright who? This is Brat," I replied, which of course was a lie.

"That is not Brat," she said.

Caught! She was caught! I got her! I got something! I felt a sudden rush of exultation. This strange woman knew Brat. If she said, *That is not Brat,* she knew.

"I assume you know," I said coolly, "that Louis Montag is dead, as is his cat-walker."

"I know."

"And the cat has vanished."

She didn't reply to this.

"Is this Bright a name? A really existing cat?"

She didn't answer.

"Please, you must help me."

"Why? Are you with the police?"

"No." I moved closer to her and tapped the scar that was still visible on the right side of my forehead, by the hair line: "I was in the apartment that night. I was almost murdered too."

She suddenly looked confused, hesitant.

I pushed on. "I am working with people who loved Louis Montag and don't believe the police will find his killers."

She smiled in an ugly fashion. "Do you think I didn't love Louis Montag? Do you think I don't mourn his death? Do I look like a woman who doesn't want his murderer caught? Listen, stranger, Louis and I were lovers for six years. Before my husband got ill, while he was ill, and after he died. Louis was my life. And I was his."

I realized of course that by chance I had hit the mother lode. But her revelation was so sudden, so complete, and so pregnant with possibilities that I did not know how to proceed.

And that word she had called me — stranger — was unnerving. In my imagination the woman in front of me suddenly took on the visage of a biblical matriarch. Who else uses such terms as stranger, or allied terms like pilgrim, sister, traveler, sojourner?

"Come in," she said.

I walked in. She closed the door. She pointed to a chair. I sat down. The apartment was small and cluttered.

Pia Jonas sat down across from me, fiddling with her hairpins.

"When was the last time you saw Louis Montag?" I asked.

"A year ago, on the street. We said hello and walked on."

"So after the affair ended, you didn't remain friends."

"No. That was impossible with Louis. He didn't know the meaning of friendship. It was not intense enough for him."

"Why did the affair end?"

"I don't know. I never knew. After Jimmy died . . . my husband, of liver cancer . . . I thought the thing with Louis would never end. I thought we would marry. But that did not happen. How sad that is! When our love was illicit, it thrived. When it was made proper by my husband's death, it disintegrated."

"What did your husband do?"

"He was a sculptor." She got up, went to a drawer, thrashed through some papers, and came back with a packet.

The first thing she gave me was a gallery booklet. It was of one of her husband's shows. In the early 90s. This particular show featured large wooden structures that looked like prehistoric birds.

I handed it back to her. "Did you know anyone who hated Louis Montag?"

"No."

"Do you have any idea why he was murdered?"

"No."

"The police believe he had something valuable in his apartment and was tortured and murdered for it. Do you know what they're talking about?"

"No. He was a reclusive man who never made a great deal of money. He did make a living from that guide book of his, but that's about all."

"Did you know Ginger Petrie?"

"No."

Then she handed me another object. It was a photograph of a beautiful large orange shorthaired tabby mama lying on her side and nursing seven tiny orange tabby kittens.

"This is Bright and her litter."

"When was this taken?"

"About five years ago. Just before my husband got sick."

"And one of the kittens is Brat?"

"Yes."

"This photo was taken in Montag's loft?"

"No! No! You have it all wrong. Bright

was Jimmy's cat, and mine. The litter was ours. They lived here. But when Jimmy got sick, Louis agreed to take them and care for them. He told us he would keep Bright and Brat and place the others in good homes. In fact he placed them all. He kept only Brat."

"They are beautiful," I said, handing the photo back to her.

"And unique," she said.

There was something about that declaration that made me nervous, although in truth everything about Pia was a bit nerve-wracking.

"All litters are beautiful and unique," I replied.

"No. I mean physically."

"How so?"

"Toes. Bright had six toes on her back feet. And so did all her kittens."

For some reason I burst out laughing. A few minutes later I left.

CHAPTER 7

The next day there was another meeting of our group — The Select Committee for the Investigation of the Murders of Louis Montag and Ginger Petrie; and the Grievous Wounding of Alice Nestleton; and the Disappearance of the Orange Tabby Cat Brat.

The meeting was held once again at the offices of Hermes Press in the Flatiron Building.

I drily detailed the substance of my conversation with Pia Jonas.

While I tried to keep my voice uninflected, it was in essence a bravura monologue, since I included everything — language, nuance, milieu. I spoke ever so drily, as I said, and I held my audience on the edge of their seats. Except for Alan Petrie, who was, as usual, standing. Did that boy never sit?

When I finished there was a long silence.

"What does it mean?" Ray Fields finally asked.

"I don't know," I replied.

The moment I uttered those words I realized I had made a serious error. I could see my reputation as the Cat Woman deflating in their eyes, quickly . . . very quickly . . . like a small balloon with a big hole.

"Look," I said, "what that woman told me might have great significance. Or it might mean absolutely nothing. The information will have to be sifted and explored, piece by piece. The affair she had with Montag. The dead husband. The six-toed cats. Everything."

"Who is going to do the sifting?" queried Noelle.

"I think, first of all, the Pia Jonas information should be relayed to the NYPD," I said.

They seemed to be in total agreement with that.

I added: "And we should all continue our work. In fact, intensify it."

"What work?" Ray asked.

"The canvassing, the digging, the inquiries. Like we did the other afternoon and evening. It turned out to be very productive — didn't it? Now we just change the questions."

Ray and Noelle immediately protested. They could not, right now, at this time, really give any more time to the investigation. Maybe later on. Alan, by his silence, seemed to support them.

It was very bizarre. After all, they had persuaded me to begin and lead the investigation. Already they were weary and wary of it. After only one excursion. The worm had turned at supersonic speed.

Well, I was not about to fight them.

Ray said: "Give me a few days."

I replied, "Of course. Call me when you want to proceed."

Then I used Noelle's office phone to contact Detective Lorenzo. I gave him the basic details of my conversation with Pia Jonas. I also gave him her address. He wanted to know the circumstances surrounding my meeting with her. The existence of the now disbanded investigatory group I did not disclose. After the call, we all sat around for about thirty minutes. Ray and Noelle reminisced tearfully about their lost friend, Louis Montag.

Then I went home. I was beginning to sense that they were all about to wash their hands of the whole thing.

And to be honest, I didn't care. But there was one problem that kept eating at me during the next few days — the six-toed cats.

Now, extra toes on cats, or strange configurations of toes, are not uncommon. However, a mother cat and a seven-kitten litter, all having six toes on each of their back feet, is a bit odd.

I kept thinking about the litter. I kept thinking about what the cats looked like grown. All orange tabby? I kept thinking about Brat and Montag and why he kept that particular cat out of the litter and where he had placed the others.

I even went to the library one morning to research six-toeness in felines — in which breeds did it tend to occur more often, whether it was a dominant or a recessive trait, and what breeders and owners thought about six-toeness. But instead of finding the answers to those questions, I ended up reading a field study of Sumatran leopards.

It was right after returning home from the library that I got the call from Sam Tully. He wanted me to meet him in a bar on Greenwich Avenue around two.

I was so happy to hear from him that I didn't even inquire as to the purpose of the meeting, and the minute I walked inside and saw him I started talking about the peculiar fact of the six-toed litter.

When I had finished the presentation, Sam narrowed his permanently bloodshot eyes and asked, "Yeah, interesting, but what do they have to do with the murders?"

His question jolted me, because I realized that I indeed believed the six-toeness had something to do with those gruesome killings and my scar. But I simply could not admit it out loud.

My reply to his question was simply: "It is too early to say."

Sam guffawed, then moved closer to me and whispered, "Well, honey, I got something that is not too early or too late. It's ripe right now."

"What are you talking about, Sam!" I said harshly. Sometimes old characters have to be brought down to earth before they get overwhelmed by their own metaphors. Especially Sam, who used to make a living writing mystery novels. It was an occupational hazard with him — thinking metaphors were real.

Sam suddenly produced a copy of *New York by Night*. Probably the same one I had purchased on our way to the Bass Line to find the bartender Montag had argued with.

"What are you doing with that?"

Sam grinned, took a sip of whatever he was drinking, and replied, "I got us a motive, honey."

"For what?"

"For the torture and murder," he announced triumphantly, slamming the guidebook down on the bar like a card player slamming a winning trick.

"I'm listening."

"The cops think this was about some exotic treasure hidden in Montag's loft. Right? And you believe it has something to do with the missing cat. Right? But what if I told you it probably has nothing to do with anything but old-fashioned extortion?"

"I'm listening."

"Okay. There are a few simple facts everyone will agree on. In a city like New York, where there is enormous competition for the money to be made out of night life, particularly the bar scene, the survival of a joint often depends on whether it can attract tourists and visitors. Right?"

"That sounds correct."

"And the best and easiest way to attract tourists is to be listed and touted in the guidebooks that tourists read. Right?"

"Right."

"Fine. Now what if Montag extorted money from bar owners to get listed prominently in his books, or even get listed at all. I'm talking about cash-under-the-table payments. Why wouldn't Montag try to score like that? The guidebook, after a few good years, was probably going nowhere. Each new edition probably sold much less than the last one. Why not grab some cash while you can! And maybe he grabbed some cash from the Bass Line — but the payments weren't made on time and he dropped the listing as punishment."

"You mean that's what Montag and the bartender, Ted Lary, were arguing about."

"On the money, honey."

Sam's thesis took my breath away. It was so simple and elegant. It cut through all the nonsensical speculation. It sounded real.

"How do we check it out, Sam?" I asked. "I mean, Montag is dead and we can't find that bartender."

"But we know the co-author. And the editor. And they're both alive and well, and their eyes are wide open. No?"

That was how we came to be ringing Ray Fields's bell an hour later on 10th Street, in the East Village.

We should have called first; he was not there. We stood on the sidewalk and contemplated our next move.

Sam suggested we wait. I agreed. His intuition was correct. Ray Fields came into view about ten minutes later, walking slowly toward his apartment from First Avenue, pulling a full shopping cart. He was out of breath when he reached us and clearly startled by our presence. I introduced him to

Sam. They shook hands. The shopping cart was filled, I noticed, with paper goods and cleaning supplies, including a new mop head. The latter was something I needed. He didn't invite us inside.

"Something has come up," I said.

He cocked his head and smiled in an ingratiating manner, the large purple birthmark on his forehead losing its visual malevolence. There was something childlike about this middle-aged man.

I waited for Sam to speak. When he didn't say a word, I realized it was I who would be making the presentation.

"Look," I said, trying to be very matter-of-fact, "we think there is some evidence pointing to the fact that Louis Montag was less than honest in his preparation of *New York by Night*."

He stared at me quizzically. "What are you talking about?"

I gave him the bone, as my grandmother used to say. "I heard he might have sold listings in the guidebook."

"Are you insane?" he shouted. "Are you people idiots?" His fury seemed to explode. He knocked the cart on its side. "Why are you making charges like this? Why are you trying to defame Louis? And me! Get it through your heads. We never sold a single listing. We never accepted a single bribe. *New York by Night* is spotless."

Sam and I walked away quickly. We entered a coffee shop on Second Avenue and assessed our wounds.

"Real or fake?" I asked Sam when we were settled.

"You mean the clown's anger?"

"Yes . . . But why do you call him a clown?"

"I hate people who use shopping carts."

"Let's stay focused, Sam."

"Okay. What the hell does it matter if the guy was acting or not? We're not going to get any information from him. But we got another source, don't we? That editor lady, whatshername?"

"Noelle Lightner."

"What are we waiting for?"

This time I called ahead. She was at work. She would be happy to give us some time. We finished our coffee and took the bus up to 23rd Street, then walked west to the Flatiron Building.

She was waiting for us behind her desk. Sam found her immediately attractive. The old reprobate literally purred.

I was the one who made the presentation, the exact same one I had made to Ray Fields.

When I finished, she glared at us for a

while, and then her face turned into a nice smile.

"To be honest with you, upon reflection, I find it funny."

"Extortion ain't funny," Sam replied, "even if it don't lead to murder."

"Look, you're way off base. Louis Montag and Ray Fields are two of the most honest gentlemen I've ever met or worked with."

I could see that Sam was getting irritated. His attraction to Noelle was diminishing. I interceded. "Tell me, though. Did you ever get a feeling that something improper was being done in relation to *New York by Night*?"

"Even if there was something improper, and that I doubt very much, I wouldn't know about it."

"But you're the editor."

"You don't understand either me or my firm's relationship to *New York by Night*. It's not a traditional publishing relationship."

"What do you mean?" I asked.

"I'm an editor in name only. The directory is produced on disc by Montag and Fields. We buy those finished pages, then print, bind, market, and sell the book."

"You mean you aren't consulted during the compilation and writing process."

"Rarely. Louis was the whole show. He

researched it, wrote it, compiled it, proofread it. When we got the disc — it was finished."

"Then what did Fields do?" Sam asked.

She smiled at Sam. I could tell my friend was now back to purring. My, this woman had affected him.

"Well," she answered slowly, "I had much more contact with Ray than with Louis. Ray dealt with contracts and finances."

"That's all he did?"

"No. Ray had some other duties. He often scouted for the guide, taking photos and leaving questionnaires for the bar owners to fill out. But when a bar was chosen to be listed, it was Louis who did the in-depth interview and evaluation and the entry itself. Look, believe me. These people aren't into extortion. They are serious book people. They love their product."

That was essentially the end of the interview. But we did not leave the office for another hour because Sam Tully started one of his crazy, complex, impossible-to-follow stories about his poisonous relationship with the entire publishing industry. To my astonishment, Noelle Lightner sat there tranquilly, listening, and it seemed that she was hearing and agreeing with every word.

69

When we finally left and emerged onto the street, Sam said, "You know, that's my kind of woman."

"And I'm sure, Sam, that if you were forty years younger, you'd be her kind of man."

"Forty years? Please, honey."

We parted at 14th Street. As he left, he said to me, "I am proceeding. You understand that?" And he waved the guidebook at me. I went home to nap and console Bushy and Pancho, although, upon arriving at my loft, I realized they were not morose at all.

It was a long nap. When I awoke it was dark outside. It was hot but no longer humid.

About nine o'clock I put on a Chopin CD and started to write a letter to A. G. Roth in London. I couldn't decide whether to inform A.G. of my current investigation — if that was what it really was. I decided against it and proceeded to fill the paper with humorous questions I wished he would answer about his lunatic pursuit of Lincoln's real killer in the archives of the British Secret Service.

The sound of Bushy clawing the fabric of the sofa interrupted me.

Instinctively I reached for the rolled up ball of socks I always kept nearby to fling at him when he performed such depredations.

I found the weapon and was about to fling it when I realized that neither of my cats was clawing anything.

The noise was coming from gravel landing on the sill of one of my open windows. It did, indeed, sound like scratching.

I walked to the window and peered down onto the street. A figure stood below.

"What are you doing?" I shouted.

The figure looked up at me, his face partially illuminated in a zebra pattern by the street light.

"Throwing stones," he shouted back at me.

I realized the stone thrower was young Alan Petrie.

A rather idiotic thought rushed in — I was in the *Romeo and Juliet* balcony scene. The girl in her bedroom, the boy below. The girl is wakened by sounds in the garden. She walks out onto the balcony.

Why was I imagining such a ridiculous cliched image? The cobwebs of longing? Lost chances?

Suddenly I was profoundly embarrassed.

"Stop it!" I called down. "What are you doing here?"

He replied: "Come down, come down." And he emphasized his words with his

71

hands outstretched in supplication, dropping what stones he had in his hands in the process.

I tried to study his face from the distance and through the partial illumination.

Did he look dangerous? No. Upset, yes, but dangerous, no.

"I'll meet you down front," I called out.

And down I went, after throwing on a thin robe.

My loft was in an old industrial building. The front entrance consisted of a small ramp and a deep outdoor alcove that led to the steel front door.

The moment I walked through that door I saw Alan Petrie pressed against one wall of the alcove. I moved to the far wall. We stared at each other from a distance of five feet.

His eyes were wild. Had he been drinking? His hands were empty. His T-shirt was dirty, and his jeans were splattered with what looked like green paint. One of his sneakers was unlaced. His hair was pulled back into a ponytail.

What I saw on his face was grief.

He suddenly shouted at me, "She was an actress, like you. Everything she did was because she wanted to act."

"Calm down, Alan. Who was an actress like me?"

72

"My sister, Ginger. She waited on tables, she worked in sleazy clubs, she walked dogs, she sat with cats. She did every lousy job under the sun because she wanted to keep studying. . . . She wanted to make it in the theater."

"Okay, Alan, okay. Believe me, I know what that's like."

The boy was highly agitated, moving his weight from one foot to the other, sweat pouring down his face.

"Listen to me. I have to tell you something now. I didn't want to tell anyone but I have to. I'm sorry he's dead, but that Montag was evil."

"Evil? How so?"

"I was suspicious of him. I always was. He was doing something to my sister. Something bad. I knew it. She started to lie to me. I think that whole cat-walking thing was a lie. Once, I waited for her in that park on Forsythe Street, where she told me she took the cat every day. She never showed."

"One day doesn't mean anything, Alan."

"You don't believe me. You don't want to accept that Montag was some kind of creep — an ugly, dangerous, evil man. That was his middle name — evil."

"Alan, what did he do to your sister? You can't make wild charges. You have to specify. Don't you understand?"

"She changed."

"How? Physically? Did he beat her?"

"I don't think so."

"Did he turn her into a prostitute?"

"No."

"Then what did he do to her?"

"I can't tell you exactly. I can't say it was A, B, or C. But it was there. He changed her. He poisoned her. And I think . . . wait . . . not think, I know . . . that everything she told me about him and her was a lie. There was something terrible going on."

I stared at him, trying to understand, trying to help, trying to show him that I wanted to help, but he had to give me something concrete.

He flung his hands up in disgust and started to walk away. He was walking past me, down my side of the ramp. I stopped him with a glancing touch of my hand on his shoulder. He wheeled. And then, don't ask me how or why, suddenly we were holding each other very tightly. And things were spinning and changing very fast — from compassion to affection to desire.

And then, bewildered, I pushed him away and stepped back. And he ran.

CHAPTER 8

The morning came quickly enough. What was the matter with me? Was I in love? Ill?

I was in love with a child. In love with a silly young man who was manufacturing demons out of a murdered man and woman.

But as the morning progressed, I was not so sure. How evil had Montag been?

I made Swedish pancakes and ate them. The morning was relatively cool. Bushy and Pancho seemed content changing window perches. At around ten, poor tailless Pancho began his mad run around the apartment, fleeing from who knows what.

Usually I ignored his paranoia, but this morning it affected me. It made me nervous. I called Sam and began to pepper him with questions about whether it was possible that this man Montag was some kind of demon. Sam wasn't very responsive, but I didn't care.

Then I went into a long, adolescent-type monologue on love, aging, death, promiscuity, felines, and, well, just about everything.

When I finished, Sam said, "Sure, honey.

Now you just keep in touch."

I sat down and wondered. Events were moving fast, I thought. Then I realized what a stupid thought that was. Nothing was happening at all except that a grief-stricken young man had shown up and we had embraced. That's all.

Then, at eleven o'clock in the morning, something did happen. A phone call from Detective John R. Lorenzo. He wanted to meet me — now.

We had lunch at the Hudson Diner, three blocks from my loft. We sat down at a booth and ordered immediately — he a grilled cheese sandwich and a 7-Up, me a poached egg on an English muffin and iced tea. I wasn't hungry at all. The Swedish pancakes had stuffed me. I ordered out of politeness.

Detective Lorenzo was not wearing his rayon suit, just an open collar jersey. By the look of things he was off duty, but he was all business.

He announced: "Louis Montag was indicted about ten years ago for mail fraud and grand larceny — specifically, the forging of historical documents."

He watched me closely. I didn't know what to say. The charges — grand larceny, mail fraud, forgery — were familiar to me. One of A. G. Roth's friends, a Lincoln buff, had been arrested on the exact same charges. He had tried to sell a short note written by Lincoln to the mother of a Union soldier killed at Shiloh. Of course, he had forged the note himself. The mail fraud charges simply meant that the grand larceny — the attempted sale of a forged document — was done by mail. Sam's intuition about Montag had been right. The man was not honest.

Lorenzo continued: "It never went to trial. The key witness against him had a stroke. Montag offered financial restitution. The D.A. accepted. Montag was slapped on the wrist and given a probationary sentence."

"What kind of documents?"

"Mostly Tory letters and diaries written in New York City during the American War of Independence."

"That's a bit too exotic for my taste, Detective. Originally I'm from Minnesota."

"I spoke to Ray Fields and that woman Pia Jonas. Neither of them knows anything about Montag's forgeries. At least, so they say."

His sandwich came. He took a big bite, chewed it thoroughly, and swallowed. Then he asked, "Do you know anything about this matter, Miss Nestleton?"

I laughed. "No, I don't. But I don't think you'd believe anything I tell you. Isn't that true?"

"To be honest, Miss Nestleton, I do find it hard to believe that you only met Montag that one time."

"Well," I replied calmly, "people used to find it hard to believe that the world was round."

And that basically ended our lunch date. There was nothing more to say. He paid the bill.

I walked over to Spring Street to visit Sam.

He was drinking vodka and root beer in front of his typewriter and squeezing half lemons into the mess.

I was agitated again but this time I gave him a blow-by-blow description of my nocturnal meeting with Alan Petrie and my lunch with Lorenzo.

He was silent for a long time. Then he lit a cigarette, flopped down on the sofa, kicking his cat, Pickles, off, and droned: "So here's the way I see it now, Nestleton. One, you got fired by that committee to find Montag's murderer. Two, you've fallen for a kid half your age who isn't playing with a full deck. Three, this Montag wasn't what anyone thought he was. And four . . ."

He seemed stumped.

"I'm waiting for 'four', Sam."

"Forget four."

"Okay."

"I got a five, though. Listen up, honey."

"I'm listening."

"Make up your mind."

"About what?"

"Are we going to conduct a serious investigation or what?"

"I'd like to, Sam."

"Yeah? But why? You don't trust the NYPD?"

"I do. But . . ."

"Forget but. In or out?"

"You have to admit, Sam, it's getting very strange. This Montag, doing unnamed horrible things to Ginger Petrie. Six-toed cats. Torture. Forged letters and diaries written by traitors to the American Revolution."

"And a little *Romeo and Juliet* scene thrown in. Yeah, it's all very strange."

"My inclination, Sam, is to proceed with all possible energy and speed."

"How?"

"Are you with me?"

"Of course. But how?"

"I think it is time to get practical."

"Like keeping away from that young kid? Good, honey. Because, let me tell you something. All the players here are not to be trusted. I think they been setting you up. I think they're playing some kind of bad game. I think we ought to keep away from all of them. If you want to solve this murder, honey, do it with your head, do it alone, and do it on the facts. You get my meaning?"

"Sure, Sam. Now let's get back to the practical."

"Why not?"

"When I used the word 'practical' I meant that it's time for you to find that bartender. And I'll go to that park on Forsythe Street and try to find out if there really existed a cat named Brat, no matter how many toes he had. And a cat-walker named Ginger, no matter how debauched she was by that devil Montag."

"You're cooking now, Nestleton. See what a little infatuation does for you?"

He stood up and freshened his drink. "By the way, if I can't find that bartender after spending sixty or so years living in New York City bars, I have a serious problem. And I ought to resign."

"Resign from what, Sam?"

"I haven't the slightest idea. But it sounds good, doesn't it? A resignation from shame. Dereliction of duty in the worst manner. I'll find that Ted Lary, or you'll fish me out of the Gowanus."

Sam was getting carried away. But as I watched the old fool replenishing his vodka and root beer (one of the worst mixtures I have ever heard of), I was struck by the wisdom of his comment . . . his intuition . . . that I was being played by a whole host of people. By Ray Fields, who had recruited me and then turned on a dime. By all of them in their way. By Alan Petrie, who had suddenly shown up. By Lorenzo, who seemed to be feeding me information. Oh, yes, Sam had a very good point. Alice, shut your ears and open your eyes.

I went to that strange ribbon park that runs from Houston Street south to Division Street, bordered east and west by Forsythe and Christie Streets, respectively. As the park proceeds south, it vanishes for a moment at every cross street, and then reappears.

The park used to be a horror but recently it was rebuilt — or rather, manicured. Now the backboards had rims and the tiny playgrounds had working swings and the long lines of benches had all been repaired.

I arrived there at five-thirty in the afternoon.

Was I there because of my infatuation

with Alan Petrie? It didn't really matter. His story had to be confirmed. Facts had to be confirmed. Simple. Practical.

Was Brat "walked" in the park daily by Ginger Petrie?

Alan implied the whole notion was a fake.

I was methodical. I entered the park where it began, at its northernmost point, and walked south, showing the cat photo to everyone in the park who would listen and describing Ginger Petrie to them as best I could. In fact, the only visual of her I had seen was the photo Detective Lorenzo had shown me.

With each presentation, I repeated the mantra: "And she was carrying a cat carrier. And in the carrier was an orange tabby cat. And she always let it out."

The population at that hour was eclectic: old men and women, young Hispanic girls, winos, tourists, working people taking a rest on their way home.

Luck was with me this time. Only a few blocks into the park, where Hester Street bisects it, I was blessed. There, on the south side, after crossing Hester, I saw an old lady feeding pigeons.

I approached and made my little presentation.

The woman's face — she had not stopped feeding the pigeons while I talked — broke into a map of creases and smiles. She then shooed the pigeons away and patted the bench.

"I'm Alice," I said, sitting down.

"I'm Hetta," she replied. "Where has the girl been?"

I didn't feel like saying, "In the grave," so all I said was, "She's in trouble."

"Well!" the woman almost shouted. "I'm her friend. We always talked. Does she need food?"

It was hard to tell who or what this Hetta was. She gave off mixed signals. She could have been homeless. But maybe not. She could have been a mental patient. But maybe not. Her clothes were contradictory. Beautiful shoes but a very tattered dress. She was heavily powdered.

Hetta fed the pigeons again, then said, "But she never walked the little fella."

"Never?"

"Never."

"Are you sure?"

"We sat together and talked almost every day. Sometimes I gave her cookies. She kept the carrier on her lap. She never walked the cat. She never opened the carrier."

That was strange.

Hetta noted: "To be honest, I did look inside. He was ugly."

"Who?"

"The cat. I looked into the carrier. I pressed my nose against it. I'm talking about the cat." She shooed the pigeons away again and brightened. "If she's in trouble, I'll help. But I'm telling you, all she did was sit here with the carrier on her lap and wait for the other woman."

That jolted me. Hetta suddenly took a straw hat out of her bag and rammed it down on her head. It was becoming obvious to me that Hetta was not as old as I'd thought initially, but she was a whole lot crazier. Still, I believed her.

"What woman?" I asked.

"I don't know. She was fat. She had funny hair. She came into the park and took the carrier, and then the girl left. And the next day the girl would come back and get the carrier back from the fat lady."

"Wait, Hetta, wait. I want to make sure I understand what you're saying. Do you mean the girl came into the park, gave the cat in the carrier to that other woman, and left empty-handed?"

"That's right."

"Where did the other woman go with the carrier?"

"She walked that way," said Hetta, pointing east.

"And the next day the girl would come into the park empty-handed?"

"That's right."

"And the woman you called the fat woman would return and give her the carrier back?"

"That's right."

"Was it the same carrier?"

"Don't know."

"Was the same cat inside?"

"Don't know."

"Was any cat inside?"

"Don't know."

That was the end of the interview. I walked back befogged. If what Hetta had told me was true, I was at Montag's that night on some kind of wild goose chase . . . on some kind of false pretense . . . on some kind of malevolent hustle. He had lied to me to get me up there. Ginger was not walking that cat. She never walked the cat. And the fat woman probably had the cat. Not Ginger . . . and therefore not Montag. Why would Montag want me up there if there was no cat to sit for? And why the elaborate cat-walking myth? Just a cover for Ginger Petrie to sit in the park and wait for that fat woman? And what was the carrier hand-off all about?

When I arrived home there were three messages on the machine from Alan Petrie.

His voice was pathetic — a lovesick puppy.

I was even more pathetic listening to his voice. I knew I could not return his call. It would be too dangerous. The child had melted me. I had become the older-woman seducer . . . the one every mother worries about when it comes to her son.

As befogged and confused and ashamed as I was — or maybe because of that — I suddenly longed to hear Sam's derelict dialect. But there was no message from him at all.

CHAPTER 9

I didn't hear from Sam the next day either.

I started to get worried by the evening. Why hadn't he called me? He was supposed to keep in touch. I kept calling his place but there was no answer.

I did get three more calls from Alan, which I did not answer, staring stonily at the instrument as it recorded. In one of them he said, "You'll never guess where I am. At the Lincoln Center library. I just looked up Nestleton, Alice, in the performing arts index. I found reviews of all the plays you ever appeared in. What do you think of that? You think I'm a fool? Maybe. I don't know why they call you the Cat Woman. I don't like the name. I think you're beautiful."

And I did get a call from my agent.

Her, I talked to. It wasn't a role in a play. She wanted to know if I would audition for a voice-over in a series of information spots for the New York City Department of Parks. It was kind of amusing, given my latest adventure in the Forsythe Street Park. Not much money, my agent said, just scale — and something that looks good on a resume.

"Of course," I said.

"I'll get back to you," she said. Which was what she always said.

The day wore on. Interspersed with my worry over Sam and my confusion about what I had learned in the park was the consistent longing I had for Alan Petrie.

It bothered me. Had I really become a seductress of young men? Although I had once made a fool of myself over a violent young man in a beach resort, this was not my usual style.

Why did I want to see him so badly? To console him? To hold him?

It couldn't be just sex. And if it was predominantly an erotic craving, then did it border on incest?

Or was it possible, simply, that I had fallen in love with a man so young, so outside my usual milieu, that I had to construct all kinds of elaborate excuses to deal with the infatuation?

But oh, the longing was there — bitter, wet ripples.

What an incredible, inexhaustible mess this Montag had made. A murderous mess that seemed impossible to mop up because it kept on spreading, like spilled milk.

Near midnight, as I was brushing Bushy — my Maine coon cat loved these nocturnal assignations — the buzzer rang.

I panicked. It had to be the boy. I didn't answer. He kept on ringing. I kept still.

And then the boy leaned on the buzzer and the loft was filled with that incessant, screeching drone.

I had to let him in the front door.

I rushed to the landing. I would yell at him to go back before he reached my landing. I would truly scream. He would get the picture.

It was not Alan. It was a disheveled, exhausted Sam Tully.

"What the hell is the matter with you, Nestleton?"

"I'm sorry, Sam, come on up."

He collapsed onto my sofa once he was inside.

"I need food and whisky, and I need them fast," he moaned.

I made him a sandwich with one slice of Swiss cheese and one slice of ham and some excellent mustard. I had no whisky at all.

He ate the sandwich like an old wolf.

"Coffee, Sam?"

"Of course, of course."

I made him espresso. He poured a huge amount of sugar into each of the three cups he drank, and then said, "I've been moving and shaking, honey. Moving and shaking and investigating."

89

"You look like you have."

"I found Ted Lary! No! As you were! I mean I found out where he used to work, before he got the job at the Bass Line on Fourteenth. The place where I gave Montag your number."

"Where?"

"Habana Blue."

"I never heard of Havana Blue."

"No, honey. Not Ha*va*na. Ha*ba*na, with a B."

"Okay. Where is it?"

"You mean where *was* it."

"Okay."

"Up on Columbus, around Ninety-eighth Street. It burned down three years ago. A bad kitchen fire, they think. Ugly scene. Three people dead."

"I don't remember hearing about it."

"That's the way it goes in this town, Nestleton. You should know that by now. A fancy bar or restaurant fire, you hear about. Habana Blue was not fancy; it wasn't even funky enough to be hip."

"Was this Ted Lary hurt?"

"No. He walked away from it. And so did the owner — a guy named Manny Soma."

"I'm confused, Sam. Did you find Ted Lary? Did you get this information from him?"

"No, honey. I didn't find him. I got all this by bugging fifty some odd bartenders up and down Manhattan Island. That means fifty or so bottles of beer. You see why I'm hungry? You see why I need some whisky?"

"You're a good man."

"Well, thank you, Nestleton. But the best is yet to come. I mean, I know you like weird stuff."

"Is that what you think of me?"

"No offense, honey. Just joking. Take a look."

He handed me *New York by Night*. It was open to a specific page.

While I held the book, he tapped an entry on that page.

It was an entry for Habana Blue.

"Is this an old edition, Sam?"

"No. The new one. The newest one. Hot off the press. The one you bought."

I read the entry carefully. It was like all the other ones in the book — name, address, phone number, price range, clientele, jukebox, description of interior. And then a passage about, how shall I put it, the general ambience. In this specific entry there was no description of entertainment or menu because Habana Blue did not provide those services.

I said to Sam, "It treats the bar as if it's still in existence. But it burned down three years ago. That doesn't make sense."

"It definitely doesn't."

"Maybe it's an editorial error. They just forgot to delete it," I speculated.

"Maybe. But take a look at that coded symbol."

To help readers, at the top of each entry was a symbol in parentheses.

"(A)" meant there was just a bar.

"(AF)" meant the place also served food.

"(AFE)" meant there was also live entertainment.

In the case of Habana Blue, there was simply: (N).

But nothing in the user's guide in the book gave any clue to what "(N)" stood for.

"Maybe," I suggested, "we ought to speak to Montag's associates."

"Come on, Nestleton. After our extortion charges, those people wouldn't give us the right time."

Sam was right. But I kept staring at the entry. How could such a mistake have passed by editorial checking for three years? Was it purposeful? Why?

"Tell me what happened in that park," Sam said, then added, "You know, I think the name of the park is Sara Delano Roosevelt. But I never heard anyone call it that, and to be honest, I don't know who this Sara was, except that she was a Roosevelt."

I told Sam about Hetta and her information.

He seemed to be absorbing it, making faces as he did so. Then he said, "Did you notice, Nestleton, that every time we make a good investigative step we open up a new can of worms? And we can't even identify what kind of slithering things they are."

"It is disheartening," I agreed.

He burst out laughing.

"What's so funny?"

"I can't figure out what to do next. I can't even figure out what Harry Bondo would do next."

"Maybe, Sam, we should get an ally."

"Where are you going with this?"

"I mean, ask yourself, who loved this man? This Montag."

"Well, Ray and Noelle seem to have been close to him. They were the ones who asked you to help them find the killers. But they didn't really love him. Right? I mean, the minute they had to do a little hard work, they bowed out. Right? Fake love. The cat girl who died probably loved him. But she can't help us now. The kid you're having the problem with, her brother, hated him.

Right? So where does that leave us? Detective Lorenzo?"

"No. Pia Jonas. She loved him. She loved his cat. Remember, it was her cat originally."

"But you already talked to her. So did Lorenzo."

"But now we have a few more questions to ask, don't we? Like the mysterious fat lady who kept taking Ginger's carrier and then returning it to her. And this Habana Blue."

"Okay. You sold me. Jonas must know some strange things. Hell, she gave away a whole litter of six-toed cats, didn't she?"

"I am thinking of a quiet, intimate dinner," I said. "Just the three of us."

Pia Jonas accepted my invitation eagerly. That was something I did not expect.

We took her to a Belgian restaurant on Lafayette Street that features dozens of exotic mussel dishes and a hundred and one monastery-brewed beers, none of them inexpensive by the glass.

We sat at a spacious table in very comfortable chairs.

Pia Jonas wasn't wearing a housedress this time, but she still looked like a rawboned refugee from the West Virginia hills.

The pins and rubber bands were still in her thick gray hair. And she still spoke quickly and a bit raucously. In fact, she was quite refreshing.

She and Sam liked each other instantly. I suppose that often happens when two oddballs meet.

After we ordered, she said to me — and to Sam, I suppose: "Why don't we get the bad part over first? The interrogation. Okay? Like Detective Lorenzo. He made it short and sweet. Did I know Louis Montag was a thief and a forger? I told him the truth — I didn't. And I don't believe it. Did I know that he was interested in that old stuff about New York City? Of course. We were lovers. Yes, I liked that Lorenzo. He got the point."

She and Sam picked up their beer steins and toasted "getting the point."

Sam looked at me. I nodded. Let him make the first move.

He pulled out the guidebook and laid it open on the table. He tapped the entry for Habana Blue.

"Would you take a look at this?"

Pia Jonas leaned over and read it dutifully.

Sam asked, "Did you ever go to that place? To Habana Blue?"

"No."

"Did Montag ever go there?"

95

"How should I know? He never took me there. He never mentioned it."

"Do you know a bartender named Ted Lary?"

"No."

"Are you sure you never heard the name Habana Blue?"

"I never heard of it."

"What about Manny Soma?"

"Who is he?"

"The owner of that bar."

"Don't know him."

"Did Montag confide in Ray Fields?"

"I don't know."

"What about his editor, Noelle Lightner?"

"Are you asking me if he confided in her? I don't know."

"Did they drink together?"

"I don't know. I never met her. I think I met Ray once."

Sam closed the book. He and Pia took another swig of their beers.

There was something kind of charming about this rawboned lady who, after living in New York for probably more than half her life, still looked and acted as if she had walked out of some coal town. Maybe it was the enthusiastic bluntness of her speech and the fact that even if she was talking directly to you, the bluntness did not seem aimed against you. Pia Jonas had a natural ability to do what many actors spend years trying to achieve — ignore the audience so that the audience, in its perversity, becomes obsessed with the actor. It is one of Stanislavski's axioms.

Then it was my turn. I told her what had happened in the park, about what Hetta had told me.

"It makes no sense at all to me," she replied. "But I never met the cat-walker. I didn't know her. I don't even know if she was around when I was going with Louis. He didn't have any cats then. Not at the beginning. I gave him the litter when my husband's health started failing."

The mussels came. We shared them. We ate and drank with some enthusiasm. Sam and Pia talked a lot. And then she made the mistake of asking Sam what he did for a living. He started telling her about his fictional detective and his now dormant mystery series.

I simply couldn't bear to hear the whole sad, confusing story again, so I asked Pia Jonas, "How did you originally meet Montag?"

She put her fork down, and her eyes misted over.

"It was a very funny meeting. Bright was about to give birth. I took her to my vet, who was then on East Ninth Street. It was a very hot day. The poor cat was screeching. The carrier was very heavy. I was at the corner of Houston and the Bowery, and suddenly I just couldn't cross that big street. A man popped out of nowhere, a tall man, offered me his arm, picked up the carrier, crossed with me, took me to a frankfurter vendor, and bought me a cold drink. He said, 'You ought to wear a hat in this weather. For the sun.' "

She picked up her fork, smiling.

"So?" Sam asked.

"So that is the way we met."

"And how did it proceed?" Sam asked.

She laughed. "Like all affairs. And we walked."

"Walked?" I asked.

"Yes. We made love and we walked. That's all we did."

"Where did you walk?" Sam asked, then added, "Oh, you mean you helped him scout for the guidebook."

"No. His partner, Ray, did most of that. Louis took me all the way downtown, mostly. Like I told the detective, I never knew about any forgeries, but I surely knew about his passion for early New York City history. That's what all our downtown walks were about. Along the southern tip of Manhattan, where the early town was, where all the docks and piers and wharves and taverns were. We would be standing in front of a huge skyscraper on Water Street or William Street and he would be talking as if the buildings weren't there and we were back in 1770 looking for some ale and pudding."

"That's funny," Sam said.

"What's funny?" I snapped.

"That none of this love for old New York shows up in his guidebook. I mean, that guy Fields might have scouted for the book, but Montag wrote the entries."

"It is strange," Pia agreed, "because he really loved old New York bars."

"You mean existing old bars, like Pete's Tavern on Irving Place?"

"No. I mean the taverns of Colonial times. He used to point out where each one had been. The names of the owners. How they got and lost their licenses. Which ones were also brothels. Which ones had Loyalist sympathies and which Revolutionary sympathies. Which were gathering places for Masons, which for privateers, which for thieves. He used to recite all their names. Old Pye House. Black Horse. Orange Tree.

Rum and Roses. Sign of the Prince of Orange. Oh, God, listen to me! I remember all of them also."

Suddenly enthusiastic, Sam asked, "What about Potter?"

"You mean Hiram Potter? Oh, Louis talked about him all the time."

I was confused. "Who is this Potter, Sam?"

"A famous eighteenth-century New York City tavern owner. My friend Turk used to talk about him. You know Turk, don't you, Nestleton?"

I nodded yes, but I really didn't know the man. I had heard of him but never met him. And to be honest, I never wanted to meet him. He was one of Sam's drinking buddies. I remember that I once asked Sam after he mentioned him, "Is the man Turkish?" Sam said, "Of course not." "Then how did he get that name?" I asked. Sam said he didn't have the slightest idea.

Pia Jonas repeated the name wistfully. "Yes, Hiram Potter. Hiram Potter. What was the name of his tavern?"

"The Red Hog," Sam answered wistfully. He turned to me and said, "You know why Hiram Potter is famous? Because what happened to him was so sad. He made a will. He left his son all his prized possessions. The

100

tavern. His Bible. A clavichord with four stops. Even his damn cat. The Red Hog burned to the ground with Hiram, the Bible, and the clavichord in it. Only the cat survived, and that's the only thing his son got."

The rest of the dinner was gloomy. My questions had led Pia into a nostalgia that inexorably turned depressive. She didn't want to say anything more about Louis Montag. But it was too late not to think about him.

In a sense, though, the dinner was a success. It hadn't really helped our investigation, but the good woman's memories had fleshed out Louis Montag for me, even humanized him.

As we left the Belgian place, Sam announced to Pia that the moment he got his next check he would like to take her on his own personal bar tour of New York City.

The woman was kind enough to say she'd be delighted. Of course, it would be a very cold day in hell before she went with him.

As Sam and I stood in front of the restaurant and watched the woman walk south on Lafayette Street, he said, "You did pick up on that contradiction, didn't you, honey?"

"Refresh my memory."

"Louis Montag spends every leisure

minute haunting the places where old bars once existed. Yet he makes a living writing guidebooks about currently existing bars and they don't say one word about the historical significance of those sites. Nothing whatsoever. You get the point? It's more than a contradiction, Nestleton. The thing is lousy with possibilities."

"Yes," I admitted. But what I really was thinking was that Sam liked this Pia so much that he was beginning to sound like an academic. Poor Sam.

To bring him back to earth, I asked, "Do you think she was lying?"

"About what?"

"Well, for one thing, about never knowing or meeting Ginger Petrie."

"I get the feeling, Nestleton, that she is unable to lie. She's like me, when I was a kid. No one could teach me to swim. I was unable to swim. But I could float."

CHAPTER 10

During the next forty-eight hours I received many calls from both Sam Tully and Alan Petrie.

The former calls I answered; the latter I did not pick up.

Poor Sam had obviously become obsessed with the contradiction that Pia Jonas had revealed — i.e., an ahistorical guidebook written by a history-obsessed author.

And Sam now was beginning to think that Ray Fields was complicit in the whole mess.

Sam kept saying that I had to go with him to consult the barfly Turk Tolchin, his friend, who seemed to know, according to Sam, even more than Montag about such legendary bartenders as Hiram Potter and his tavern, the Red Hog.

I said to him, "Sam, I thought we knew what we have to know about the Red Hog. It's a children's story with a moral. A man makes a will leaving his most treasured possessions to his son. Everything goes up in flames, including the father. And the only thing the will can pay off on is the thing the son treasures least — the bar cat. I get the picture, Sam. I don't know how many more details I want. I'm not Montag."

He protested, "There were many other Potters in Colonial America, honey, a lot of them more interesting."

Defeated, I said I would accompany him shortly.

He kept calling with newer and newer twists and more urgency. He added Noelle Lightner to his list of suspects arising out of the contradiction.

Finally I let the machine take his calls, just like Alan's.

Then, on the second evening of that forty-eight-hour span, I received another call from my agent. "Go to sleep early tonight, Alice," she said. "The audition is tomorrow at nine in the morning."

I had totally forgotten what I was supposed to audition for. She enlightened me: voice-over spots for the New York City Department of Parks.

To make a long story short, I showed up the next morning at the offices of Dubnow and D'Alia, the advertising agency handling the Department of Parks account. I was treated quite well — as were the seven other women there to audition — ushered into a sound chamber type room, and given a brief script to read. It was about the return of the red-tailed hawk to Central Park.

One of the technicians confided to me that he'd seen me in an Ibsen play years ago at a theater on the same block as the famous Off-Broadway theater La Mama. He didn't remember the name of the play or the theater but he said I was *wonderful*.

The whole thing was over in forty minutes.

And then I was on Lexington Avenue and 40th Street at ten in the morning.

It was one of those delicious late-summer mornings in the city — warm, dry, windy, pregnant with the coming change of season.

I started to walk slowly downtown. I thought that what I would like to do is see a movie, a good movie. Easier said than done. I had been finding most of the current crop unwatchable.

The paper, however, which I obtained from a newsstand on Thirty-fourth and Lexington, noted that *Lovers on the Bridge* was playing at my neighborhood art house, the Film Forum.

That was a French movie a few years old. It was supposed to be good. The paper said the first showing was at one o'clock. That was ideal. I could stroll all the way downtown, stopping off for a salad on Sixth Avenue. A long walk and a green salad would clear my mind, no question about it.

And then a good movie.

The beginning of the plan went perfectly.

At twelve-fifty I was reading the glowing review of *Lovers on the Bridge* (originally titled *Les Amants de Pont Neuf*) reproduced in the theater lobby. The film was about two homeless, borderline psychotics — a man and a woman — who meet while sleeping on a condemned bridge over the Seine. Their affair, the reviewer said, was both "coruscating and liberating."

My, my, what a combination.

I turned and stared out the highly polished glass doors onto the street. Instead of the street, I saw myself clearly in the glass. Even the scar was visible.

The ticket seller was only five feet away, but I didn't make a move toward the booth.

I suddenly realized I didn't want to see a movie. And I didn't want to think about a criminal investigation. I felt bewildered. Was it sunstroke from the long walk downtown?

All I really wanted to do was see Alan Petrie.

I wanted to *see* him. I wanted to talk to him, listen to him, console him.

Above all, I wanted to hold him again.

I walked back to my loft. I ignored Bushy and Pancho. I waited.

Ten, fifteen, twenty minutes. Oh, he would call again, soon.

An hour passed.

The phone rang. I picked it up and shouted, "Yes!"

There was silence. I knew it was the boy. Why did I keep calling him a boy?

He finally spoke: "I have been calling you for days. Why didn't you answer? Will you see me now?"

"Yes."

"Where?"

"Anywhere you want."

"Tonight. Will you see me tonight?"

"Yes."

"Where?"

"Do you want to come here, Alan?"

"How can I believe you? How do I know you aren't just saying this to get me off the phone? How do I know you don't fear me and loathe me?"

"I don't have any reason to lie to you."

"Well, I don't want to go to your place again."

"Okay."

"I'm staying at my sister's. On Twenty-sixth and Ninth. It's a mess. I'm ashamed to bring you up here. And I'm scared."

"Scared? Why?"

"I'm not supposed to be staying here."

"Then come here."

"No! I'll tell you what to do. Across the street from me is a fruit market. I can see it from my window. Be there at nine tonight. I'll look out. If you're there, I'll come down. We'll find a place to go."

"Like Romeo and Juliet, Alan?"

"No. Like you and me. Will you be there? Do you promise to be there? Do you swear you'll be there?"

He was acting like a child again. But I could not fault him.

"Nine o'clock, Alan," I said, and hung up.

I could not describe how I felt after that call until I remembered that review of *Lovers on the Bridge* — "coruscating and liberating."

Over the next few hours I oscillated between them.

Eight p.m. How does a forty-one-year-old woman dress for an assignation with a twenty-year-old man?

Wide-leg gray cotton trousers with an elastic waist. Black leather sandals and a long black Indian style blouse.

I let my hair fall down and brushed it out.

Was it really an assignation? I have never fully understood what that word meant.

Assignations, of course, were what the lovers on the bridge had. Any lovers on any bridge. And they were all coruscating and liberating.

I entered the summer night at eight-twenty.

I took a bus up to 23rd, walked the rest of the way, and located the fruit stand quickly. It was just west of Ninth, on 26th Street. Not many of them on side streets like this one.

I stationed myself at the west end of the stand, almost against the building, next to the melons (expensive) and the blueberries (cheap).

Across the street were old five-story buildings, one after another, flush against one another, four windows for each floor in each building. There were lights in some of the windows and others were dark.

Alan could be looking out of any one of them.

I asked the man tending the fruit what time it was. Almost nine, he said. Then he gave me a long, suspicious look and went back to his work. He was straightening a jumble of grapes, forming them into pyramids in the box.

I waited. This was, I thought, an absurd assignation. I am waiting for a young man to peer down at me, to confirm that I did not lie to him, that I kept my promise.

But I must confess, there was a certain romantic and illicit charm about it. Alice Nestleton as a Chelsea streetwalker.

I let my eyes run along the windows. I wondered if I was standing in a spot with enough light to be seen from across the street.

I waved at the windows.

Then I heard a sound. My eyes instinctively moved toward it. The sound was distinctly musical.

Then I saw Alan.

He seemed to be waving to me as he hurtled through the shattered glass and fell at the speed of thirty-two feet per second to the street below.

I cannot describe the horror of that sound when Alan hit the concrete.

And I cannot describe my feelings or actions during the next thirty minutes.

Gradually I became aware that I was seated in the back of an FDNY ambulance with its doors open, and a medical technician standing outside was asking me: "Do you want to go to a hospital, miss?"

A new face appeared, a familiar one.

"Do you know me, Miss Nestleton?"

"Yes."

"What is my name?"

"I don't know."

"They found my card in your purse. You were in shock. I'm a cop, Miss Nestleton. Don't you know my name?"

"Romeo," I said.

"No. Lorenzo."

He helped me out of the van and into the back of an unmarked police car. He told me to relax and wait there. He said he would be back soon. Of course I would wait for him. Where could I go?

I sat there for a long time, my eyes closed, my back straight against the seat.

Lorenzo returned with a man he introduced as Detective Healy. They both slid into the front seat.

Healy stared at me through the mirror. Lorenzo turned around and stared directly at me.

"Do you want something cold to drink?" he asked.

"No." I wasn't hot. If anything, I was cold.

"Are you sure you don't want to go to the hospital?"

"I'm sure."

"Did you see him fall?"

"Yes."

"What the hell were you doing there?"

"Waiting for him."

"You're lying."

"No."

111

"The Korean man saw you signal someone. Who were you signaling?"

"I waved, that's all. It wasn't a signal."

"You lied to me about your relationship to Montag, and you're lying now."

"No. You don't understand. I had a date with Alan Petrie. He told me to wait for him downstairs. He didn't want me to come up to the apartment . . . it was his sister's. So I waited. And then I saw him fall."

"Are you sure he fell?"

"You mean perhaps it wasn't Alan?"

"Oh, it was him all right. But he might have been pushed."

I couldn't keep up with the barrage of questions and answers. I wanted him to leave. I wanted to hit him. I wanted to shut him up.

"You signaled to someone," he said again.

I didn't answer.

"Was that kid a threat, lady? Could he tie you to the Montag murders? Was that it? You were signaling to your partner in Petrie's apartment. Do you like killing young men, Miss Nestleton?"

I didn't answer.

Lorenzo cursed and got out of the car.

"Drive her home," he said in disgust to Detective Healy.

CHAPTER 11

Forty-eight hours later I was sitting in one of Sam's sleazy bars. I needed a friend. I was drinking gin and tonic and talking a blue streak.

My conversation was not about anything. It wasn't even a conversation — rather a babbling monologue about everything and nothing.

After my third drink I drifted into silence.

Sam kept me company, patient, saying little.

Then I began to speak to him with some logic. The bar was very dark and a bit warm. The jukebox was playing, believe it or not, old Patti Page songs.

"If it was suicide, Sam, there can be only two reasons."

"If you say so, honey."

"The first reason: He was in love with me and believed I would not reciprocate. He didn't see me next to the fruit stand. He jumped to his death out of despair. Young people do it all the time, especially after they have lost a loved one. Love kills. Especially unrequited love."

"But what if he saw you there and just

wanted you to see him die?"

"Why would he do that? If he saw me, that meant I would return his love."

"Maybe the kid was insane."

"Don't say that, Sam."

"Were you really there to return his love, Nestleton?"

"I think I was. Please don't laugh at me, Sam."

"I'm not laughing. You said there might have been another reason for suicide."

"Yes. Reason number two: It was his way of confessing."

"To what?"

"To the murder of Montag. Maybe he wanted to jump just before I got there. Maybe he wanted me to find his body. Maybe he thought I would immediately remember what he told me — how Montag had demonized his sister — and I would know his suicide was a confession that he had indeed taken his revenge on Montag."

"And the second man?"

"What second man?"

"The cops seem to think it was two people who entered the loft that evening after clobbering you at the door. Two people who tortured and hung Montag."

"True, they do think that. But they don't know for sure."

"You're not hinting that this Alan was so bent on revenge that he also killed his sister? He killed the debauched, even though he loved her, as well as the debaucher?"

"Of course not. But maybe Ginger Petrie was killed before Montag. Alan could have discovered that fact. Maybe Montag himself killed her sometime before I got to his loft."

"Okay, honey, slow down. Let's take a different tack. What if Alan was pushed out that window?"

"Then we're back at square one. The bodies keep falling, and we don't know why."

"Who'll be next?"

"I don't know. It could be anyone, since we have no motive."

"It could be Noelle Lightner."

"Sure, Sam. Or it could be me."

I lay my head down on the bar. I wondered what A. G. Roth or Tony Basillio could say about this doomed love.

There were six or seven other patrons in the bar. All of them alone, silent, glum, and/or inebriated.

Sam broke the quiet. "To be honest, honey, it is the sister I have been thinking about."

"Why not? She appears to have been a

lovely young woman. Too young and too lovely to die like that."

"Remember you told me Alan talked about how she took all kinds of jobs?"

"That's par for the course. The girl wanted to act."

"Right."

"What if she worked at Habana Blue?"

It was one of those connections that I had never thought of. I sat up straight and peered through the smoke wreathing Sam's face.

"What made you think of that, Sam?"

"I don't know."

"It's an exciting speculation," I noted. Indeed, it seemed to open the floodgates of my mind.

Sam laughed at my pomposity. I ordered a cup of coffee.

"You think it's plausible?" he pressed.

"More than plausible. It brings up all kinds of possibilities."

"Such as?"

"Such as, if she did work at Habana Blue, the bar and the guidebook suddenly take center stage. Maybe something to do with your original speculation . . . you remember, Sam? Extortion, you said. Anyway, we have to follow up."

"I did all I could, honey. The Habana

Blue burned down. And we can't find Lary or the owner. At least I don't know where to find them."

"Not only the people, Sam, the entry."

"We're not connecting."

"You know, the strange symbol next to the Habana Blue entry in *New York by Night*. The letter in parentheses."

"I'm with you now."

"We never checked if there were other similar entries."

"Well, get the book out, honey!"

He thought for a minute. "It has to be at my place."

A half hour later, he and I were walking into his apartment.

Sam flicked on the light and let out a bellow like the water buffalo he aspires to be.

The table that held his typewriter, notes, pencils, pads, manuscript pages, and clips seemed to have been attacked with a vengeance — trashed.

Paper was everywhere. The tabletop was a terrible mess.

Sam began to curse his cat, Pickles. I tried to calm him. No use. It was Pickles who did it. No doubt about it. He had done it before. Sam took revenge. He rushed into the kitchen, picked up the cat's bowl of dry food and flung the pellets into the air violently — every which way. It was raining pellets. Pickles was nowhere to be seen.

When Sam calmed down, he made a pot of espresso. We drank out first cups fast and turned to *New York by Night.*

I sat down in his ratty easy chair with the guidebook in my lap. He turned on the reading lamp full blast, over my right shoulder. Sam's apartment had no overhead lighting, no ceiling fixtures. There were only table and floor lamps.

He sat down on the chair by his typewriter, holding a Con Ed bill and a ballpoint pen to jot down my findings, if any.

Pickles, a cat with a weird leopard-like coat, sauntered through the open window and screeched a few times. Sam cursed him genially. The cat vanished back out the window and up the fire escape to the roof, where, as Sam put it, he hung out.

My methodology for the search was quite primitive. I went through the guidebook a page at a time, through the main listings.

I was looking for one thing only — entries with the notation "(N)."

I found the first one in the Manhattan section. I read it out to Sam: "Name, the Green Room. West Street."

Sam wrote the data down on his Con Ed

bill and said, "That's not so far from here. I remember it. Not my kind of place, but I used to pass by it all the time whenever I went to the Ear Inn on Spring Street. It was right around the corner from there."

"Is it still there?"

"No. I'm pretty sure they shut down."

I found the second (N) also in the Manhattan section and read that out too: "Name, On the Bay. East Village. Eleventh Street between A and B."

"Don't know it," he said as he wrote.

I found another (N) in Queens: "Name, Paladin. Sunnyside, Queens. Queens Boulevard.

"Do you know it?" I asked.

"I'm not sure. I think I was in it once. I used to go to Sunnyside a lot for good olives and halvah at those Syrian and Turkish delis. But I can't picture the bar now."

I went through the entire book again, even more slowly, drinking more espresso with sugar as I proceeded.

There were no more (N)s.

"Do you have a new phone book, Sam?"

He retrieved it for me. Neither the Green Room nor On the Bay was listed. Sam didn't have a Queens phone book. I called information for the number of Paladin, in Sunnyside. There was no listing.

"Three for three," Sam noted. "All out of business for whatever reason, and yet all listed in the current *New York by Night*. They join Habana Blue."

"How do we get some background on these places, Sam?"

"Turk would probably know."

There was that name again, that friend of his, the one Sam had mentioned during the conversation with Pia Jonas about the sad Colonial bartender Hiram Potter and his tavern, The Red Hog.

"Can you reach him now?" I asked.

"Maybe. What time is it?"

"Around eleven."

"I figure he'll be in the Blarney Stone on Third and Forty-fifth. Turk's old now. You can plot his bar stops. He always works from uptown toward Downtown. I figure he hit P. J. Clark's on Fifty-fifth about nine. Yeah, he oughta be in the Blarney Stone by now. Like I said, he only hits about six bars a night now."

I handed him the phone book. He made the call. He got the Blarney Stone bartender, who graciously put him through to Turk Tolchin.

Sam proceeded to converse in that exotic New York city bar dialect that is incomprehensible to anyone not in the process of having alcohol violate the blood-brain barrier.

It went on for some ten minutes. I had the remaining espresso. Finally Sam hung up.

"Okay, honey, listen. The place called On the Bay blew up — a gas explosion, they think. The one called Paladin burned down. Turk don't remember exactly when. Three or four years ago. Not longer. A couple of injuries, no fatalities."

I absorbed the information quietly.

"The coincidences are getting wilder and wilder, Nestleton."

"I agree, Sam. What do you suggest?"

"Manny Soma."

"What about him?"

"We have to figure a way to find and talk to that character. He's the man who walked away from the Habana Blue fire alive."

"Not the only one," I pointed out. "So did Ted Lary."

"Yeah, I know. But his trail is cold and dead."

I thought to myself, bitterly, that Alan Petrie's trail was also cold and dead — in a much more literal sense.

Sam went into the kitchen and tried to gather up the scattered pebbles of dry cat food.

I closed my eyes and napped. When I

awoke it was past midnight. Sam was watching me.

"You okay?"

"I'm fine," I said.

"Thinking about Manny Soma?"

"No."

"Well, I am, and I got a possibility."

"I'm listening."

"Pick up the phone and call your friend Nora."

Sam was thinking very clearly. Nora owned a bistro in the theater district. She knew everybody in the business.

Her address and phone number on Martha's Vineyard was on a slip of paper buried deep in my wallet. It took me a long time to find it.

I dialed the number. I woke her up.

"Trouble, Alice?" was the first thing she said after coming out of her daze.

"No."

She laughed. "Then you've met a man. That has to be it. You should be ashamed of yourself. A.G. in England. Tony in L.A. And you are going wild. Whatever will become of you, Alice Nestleton? You are a disgrace to the American theater. Let's face it. You need me around to look after you."

"Well, Nora, there is someone." The moment I said those words I wondered if I had lost my sanity. Yes, there might have been a man . . . there might have been.

"Alice, are you coming up here before the summer's over?"

She went into a long discourse on the beauty of the Vineyard.

I listened until she had almost exhausted the superlatives. Then I broke in. "I need your help, Nora."

"Well, why didn't you say so? Shoot."

"I need to locate a man named Manny Soma."

"Sounds familiar."

"He used to own a bar uptown called Habana Blue."

"Oh, yes. I remember it. The place that burned down. Soma . . . Soma . . . I know who you're talking about."

"Do you know how I can contact him?"

"Looking for a waitress job, dear?"

"I'm looking for information."

"About what?"

"The living and the dead."

"That just about covers everybody. Okay. I think — I'm not absolutely sure — but I think he's managing a new place in Abingdon Square. Nope."

"Nope?"

"That's what it's called — Nope. Actually, I hear they got a top chef, but the place is doing badly. It hasn't caught on."

I thanked her, promised to call again soon, and gave Sam the information.

"No more calls, Nestleton. Let's get down there."

"Now?"

"You beat?"

"Yes, I'm beat."

"We have to talk to this Soma."

"I know that."

So we went.

CHAPTER 12

One-fifteen in the morning. Nope existed. The more you thought about the name, the less stupid it sounded.

The place was elegant and empty. The menu was difficult to understand — a lot of modified Asian dishes.

Manny Soma was seated at a back table. He was fastidiously dressed — a handsome middle-aged man with thick, beautiful salt-and-pepper hair. He brought to mind a polite lion seated calmly on an empty plain.

He was so polite, so accommodating, that he didn't even ask why we were firing questions at him.

No, he didn't remember any waitress by the name of Ginger Petrie who worked at Habana Blue.

No, he was sure that no one of that description had ever worked there.

No, he never met a Louis Montag or a Ray Fields.

No, he didn't remember being interviewed for *New York by Night* at any time in any restaurant he had ever worked in or owned.

No, he didn't know where Ted Lary was

working now, but he thought it might be somewhere in Dallas.

Then Sam asked him about the fire at Habana Blue, and for the first time he seemed to lose his composure. The memory seemed to pain him greatly. He turned his pain on us.

"You walk in here like lords of the dance. You don't identify yourselves. You don't eat or drink. You give a vague reference in the restaurant business, this Nora. You sit around and pick my brains like you're collecting a loan. What the hell are you people about?"

"We're trying to right a wrong," I said.

That made Soma laugh, bitterly. "What right? What wrong? Are you talking about Habana Blue? The place went up like a match. Fast. Very fast. The fire started in the kitchen. It was a grease fire that became a firestorm. It never should have happened. But it was an accident. How are you going to right that? Raise the dead?"

He got up then and said, "Let me buy you people a drink before you leave."

We walked over to the bar with him. He signaled to the bartender, who brought out a bottle of champagne and poured three glasses.

There were no other patrons at the bar.

There was, however, a party of six drinking at a table in the L-shaped extension of the bar — not visible when one entered.

What a strange trio we were. Only Sam drank the champagne. He also ran his hand over the top of the bar and told Soma that while he kind of liked Nope's decor, he definitely didn't like the composite metal stuff used to coat the bar counter. He preferred wood.

Manny Soma replied, "I didn't design the place. I just run it."

"What does the name Nope mean?" I asked.

Soma replied, "It means what it means."

"Do you think this place is gonna make it?" Sam asked.

"Too early to tell."

The man's loquaciousness had fled. Sam asked him, "Do you think we're insurance investigators?"

Soma looked at me. "No. You're too good-looking. Besides, the insurance payout after the fire was so pitiful, the company wouldn't spend more than a first class stamp to investigate."

Sam changed the subject, bringing it back to my inquiry on the name of the place. "Maybe Nope was a mistake. Maybe it was supposed to be Hope . . . or Loop. Or maybe it's a geographical acronym — like SoHo or NoHo."

"I didn't name the place," Manny said again.

But Sam could not be stopped. "You know that post office on Hudson? Maybe Nope means north of post office."

"That would be Nopo," Soma said, looking around as if trying to find a gentle way to get us out of there.

But Sam kept on acronyming.

I looked past the bar, into the immaculate kitchen. It was obviously closed for the evening but the door was wide open, displaying the spotless work counters, ranges, and pots.

I was resigned and calm. We had located Manny Soma, and it had proved to be worth nothing, like everything else in this cursed inquiry.

Just seeing that kitchen, however, was worth the visit. It gleamed so, it was so functional, so waiting to be used . . . crying out to be used.

I was also looking for the cat. The kitchen cat or the bar cat or whatever one called him or her. All the bars and restaurants south of 14th Street on the West Side had to have at least one cat. The collapsed wharves on the Hudson and the many abandoned water mains had created a rodent nirvana.

But the beast was in hiding. I wondered what kind of a cat a posh new spot like Nope would acquire. Maybe a Siamese. Maybe a pair of them.

I peered over the elegant bar.

"What's down there?" Sam asked me.

"I'm looking for the house cat."

"We don't have one," Manny Soma said.

Sam guffawed. "In this neighborhood? You must be kidding."

"We use exterminators," Soma replied.

Sam laughed even louder.

It was time to go. I thanked Mr. Soma for his time. He invited us to dine at Nope sometime soon.

We walked out and stood in front of the place.

"Another wild night, huh, Nestleton? Wild, wild nights in the big city."

I didn't respond to his sarcasm. For some reason the fact that Nope did not have a cat disturbed me.

"You look unhappy," Sam noted. Then he added, "The breaks are just not going our way. Our luck is bad now. Who could figure? We finally get hold of this Soma and he can't tell us a bloody thing."

"Sam, listen. I have the funny feeling that he did tell us something important."

"What?"

"That he doesn't have a cat."

"Well, maybe it's just that our friend Soma knows the pathetic story of Hiram Potter. Maybe Soma would rather leave his son nothing than leave him a mangy, hexed cat."

"You mean if Nope burns down?"

"No, I mean if Soma has a son."

I didn't reply.

"Okay, honey. I did make one of my brilliant diagnoses when I was in there. I know that between the time you looked behind the bar and the time we stepped out into the air, one of those festering feline fantasies took over your cerebral cortex."

I smiled at him. "Sam, I'm not really tired anymore. These wild nights in the big city invigorate me. I'm beyond sleep. Maybe it's time I really learned about Hiram Potter and his cat."

"You mean from the Turk?"

"That is exactly what I mean."

Two-thirty a.m. Sam and I were walking toward the rear of a gloomy bar called Molly's on Third Avenue, somewhere south of 23rd Street.

Sam was sure Turk was there, that Turk had left the Blarney Stone where Sam had called him for information on the "(N)" bars in *New York by Night* at around two and was now in this place — Turk's next-to-last stop of the evening.

Sam was right.

We found him in the last booth on the right. I had expected a drooling old drunk on the verge of alcoholic psychosis, but he was much more sophisticated than that, and perfectly sane, as far as I could tell. In fact he didn't appear inebriated in a classical sense. You just knew, however, that something was very wrong with him, over and above the age and decrepitude. He breathed very hard and heavily while smoking some kind of thin, cork-tipped cigarillos.

His face was rotund and cherubic. It might have been the face of an aging, mischievous little angel, except for the trail of broken blood vessels, particularly around the nose — the sure sign of a lifetime's drinking. He had a few strands of brown hair left, and they were plastered down on the front of his head. At any rate, his appearance was a great deal neater than Sam's. Turk wore a thick flannel shirt buttoned at the collar and a flamboyantly knotted old-boys' tie. Since it was summer, the flannel shirt made no sense at all until I reasoned that this man must spend his life in heavily air-conditioned bars.

Turk spoke in a very slow, articulate manner. His voice was actually mellifluous, pedantic, as if he were perpetually giving a philosophy lecture to mentally challenged people. His accent was very posh New York.

I had no idea what he was drinking. It was a clear liquid.

The moment we slipped into the booth across from him, he said: "Tully, I'm not sure I want to talk to you anymore this evening. Calling me at the Blarney Stone was quite irresponsible. Almost vulgar. Perhaps . . . yes, perhaps even an aggressive action. Are you looking for trouble with me, Tully? Because if it's trouble you want, it's trouble you will get."

He didn't wait for an answer or even a response from Sam. He just turned his gaze on me. "So you are that woman, Nestleton. Tully has apprised me of your tastes. Sad."

I didn't know what he meant. And as I looked at him, I had no idea why anyone would want to call him Turk.

"Listen, Turk," said Sam, "she wants to hear about Hiram Potter and his cat."

"Then tell her."

"I did tell her. She wants to know more."

"Then go to the sources," he suggested.

"She doesn't have time," Sam insisted.

Turk Tolchin stared at me for a long time, twirling the cork-tipped cigarillo in his mouth as if it were a licorice stick. He seemed to be evaluating me by some exotic criteria.

Then he inquired, "What precisely is your Potter problem?"

I replied, "From what I know of the story, I don't understand why so many people are so fascinated by this Potter and his cat."

"You're exaggerating," he corrected. "Few people are fascinated by it."

"Okay. But why are they?"

He gave Sam a dirty look, took a dip of the liquid in his glass, and then relented.

"Nestletine, I don't think you come from that class of literate barflies who can truly appreciate it, but I shall try to help you . . . out of my long, difficult, and rapidly receding friendship with Tully.

"Who was Hiram Potter?" he went on. "A poor Colonial man. We don't really know, but we can reconstruct his life a bit. All conjecture, of course. Probably a woodcutter in the city. Probably graduated to tavern helper, cleaning out slops and flushing ale casks. Probably moved on to become bartender. Probably saved every penny he earned. Probably dreamed of owning his own tavern.

133

"And then one day the dream came true. He became sole proprietor of the duly licensed Red Hog. Now he was a man of property and substance . . . a tavern keeper . . . when such institutions were the political and social centers of the city.

"He had achieved petit bourgeois heaven. His wife died. He had a son whom he loved. So, like a good burgher, he decided to prepare a will, giving to his son everything he had worked for and treasured: his Bible, his bar, his clavichord with four stops. And his cat, which he didn't really treasure, but in those days every tavern needed a cat. So he threw it in as an afterthought.

"The Red Hog went up in flames a few days after he made the will. Some stories say it was a week later. Some say within twenty-four hours. Everything burned up with the tavern — Hiram, his Bible, and his clavichord with four stops.

"The only thing his son got was the mangy cat."

Sam interceded: "Don't you get it, honey? The moral of the tale?"

"Well, maybe," I answered.

Sam shouted, "Of course you do! It's simple. The moral is: Don't ever make a will."

Both men laughed.

Turk Tolchin added, "And don't take a cat who has been willed to you."

"Why not?" I asked.

"Learn! Learn from young Potter. Out of love for his father's memory, he would not relinquish the cat."

"That makes sense."

"But the cat was deformed. We don't know in what way. And the cat was very, very bad luck. A hexed cat. We don't know how, but legend has it that the cat destroyed the young man. One old lady, writing a recipe book some fifty years later, one of those gossipy books, says that Iron Betsy did it with fire and brimstone. Whatever that means."

"Did you say Iron Betsy?"

"That was the cat's name, and mayhem was her game."

"Get it, honey?" Sam asked. "All the Potters die, and only Iron Betsy survives."

"I get it, Sam. But what ultimately happened to her?"

"That," said Turk, "is one of the few things we know for sure — at least there is a written record. Iron Betsy ended up hunting rats on a British man-of-war moored in New York Harbor during the Revolution. The ship, the *HMS Blade*, burned and sank. It was thought to be sabotage by American pa-

135

triots press-ganged and forced to serve on the *Blade*. Iron Betsy was never heard from again."

I couldn't ask any more questions. I was too dumbfounded. The odd thing is, I didn't know why. It was the same feeling that came to me as I left Nope, only more intense. I was being manipulated by a nonexistent cat in Manhattan in the year 2000 and a cat from 1776, also in Manhattan.

Then Sam said to Turk, "I want you to look at something."

He took out the guidebook and opened it on the table in front of Turk. He flipped the pages until he reached one of the bar entries that Turk had given him information about — On the Bay.

Turk put on a pair of very thick glasses and peered at the entry through whatever cobwebs inhabited his brain and optical system.

"What precisely do you want me to look at?" he asked.

"The symbol in the entry."

"I see it; I am looking at it."

"Now look at the other symbols on the page. You see? They're '(A)' '(AF)' or '(AFE)'. But On the Bay has an '(N)'."

"That is correct."

"Can you figure out what it means?"

"Doesn't the author tell you?"

"No."

Turk Tolchin stared at it a long time, manipulating both his cork-tipped cigarillo and his drink as he read.

Finally he announced, "It's a game."

"Okay. How do you play?"

"It's quite simple. You free associate."

"Huh?"

"I don't have the energy to explain to you, so I'll just give you the end game. The letter N stands for either naught, naughty, nifty, nada, nihil, necrophiliac, not, nothing, nimble, nouveau, nonsensical, numinous, natty, or nautical."

Then, after that ridiculous explanation, his hand still on the open book, Turk Tolchin seemed to lapse into a coma of some sort. He was simply immobile and unreachable.

"Well," said Sam, "at least you know Iron Betsy and Hiram Potter now."

"What do I know?" I asked bitterly.

"Probably all you have to know, honey."

"I have two problems, Sam. Two things . . . two facts . . . two feelings . . . two appurtenances. To be honest, I don't know what to call them. Why doesn't Soma's restaurant, in the heart of rodent country, have a cat? And why was Louis Montag so deep into this nonsense about the Potters?"

"You sure it's nonsense?"

"Sam, I know that Hiram Potter is the patron fool of literate barflies, as your comatose friend notes. But Louis Montag wasn't a barfly, he was a guidebook writer. And so little of the Potter story is verifiable."

"Then forget about it. I brought you here because you wanted to hear about Potter and his cat. Mission accomplished."

"I know. I appreciate it, Sam. I'm not attacking you. I'm attacking myself, my unformed speculations, my denseness."

We sat there in silence. The bar was beginning to shut down.

Turk was now slumped against the side of the booth.

"What do you do with him?" I asked.

"Nothing. The bartender will put him in a cab."

"Where does he live?"

"Somewhere on West Fifty-seventh Street."

"What does your friend do for a living?"

"He's a dealer."

"Cards?"

"No."

"Art?"

"No. Just objects."

"You mean he buys and sells objects?"

"Yeah."

"What kind?"

"Large objects."

I didn't press it any further.

I took one last look at Turk Tolchin; tried to visualize a New York city circa 1776; tried to picture in my head a tavern sign reading THE RED HOG, and inside, the owner and his cat — Hiram Potter and Iron Betsy.

Futile. Maybe with an acting coach I could have done it. But not in that bar at that time with two inebriates beside me.

CHAPTER 13

I woke up petrified and drenched with sweat.

And I woke up hearing pebbles against a window. Confused, not remembering any dream, I rushed to the window and stared down onto the street.

When I realized I was looking for Alan Petrie, I felt shame and loathing and went back to bed.

Bushy and Pancho were staring at me with some curiosity.

I looked at the clock: 1:15 . . . in the afternoon.

I had slept straight through — from 4 a.m., when I finally arrived home, until now. The morning was gone, vanished, unseen.

Why weren't the cats screeching? Didn't they want their breakfast, however late? They kept staring at me — accusing but silent.

Finally I arose for good, filled their bowls, and made myself coffee. Then I took my coffee and sat down on a window ledge to stare down at the street again. Had the pebbles I'd heard upon waking been part of an Alan Petrie nightmare? Of him flinging the pebbles during that nocturnal visit? Of him hurtling through the glass to his death? I didn't remember. But there had to be some explanation for awakening to sounds that didn't exist.

Sitting there, sipping the strong black coffee, I began a rather pathetic exercise, trying to imagine what would have happened had Alan not leaped — or been pushed — to his death.

What would have happened between us? What could have happened?

I could picture only delightful scenarios. I could see us in foreign locales, lush terrains, exotic entertainment spots.

I could see us as friends and lovers.

I could see us as poster children for some kind of ideal relationship I could not name.

All this was nonsense, of course, and I realized it. There was no real reason to believe that had Alan lived, our relationship would not have been exactly like every other relationship I have ever had with a man, no matter his age: confusing, difficult, and ultimately unhappy.

Look at me now! Two men in my life, you could say — but one in England and one in Los Angeles. Both of them once and future lovers. One of them, A. G. Roth, a bit mad.

The other, Tony Basillio, a pathological philanderer.

Neither of them longed for me the way Alan Petrie had. Neither of them elicited from me the sense of illicitness that I had experienced with Alan — whether that was good or bad. Neither of them would kill for me, as Alan might have done.

I was suddenly embarrassed by the romantic tripe I was dishing up to myself. Kill for love? Poor old thespian Nestleton . . . one bad part too many.

Bushy jumped onto my lap. I shooed him off. He complained loudly and stalked away.

Sitting there, still not dressed to begin the day, I was assaulted by loneliness. One of those dreadful storms of loneliness that quickly fling you into depression, and worse. The plague that chews into your marrow, like a beast, and soon you know that all your plans, hopes, and possibilities are doomed.

Yes, that's what hit me that August afternoon.

So what did I do?

I picked up the phone and called Tony in L.A.

And the minute he picked up, I attacked. "I thought I might catch you in now, Tony. I remember that your seductions have begun to exhaust you. So you sleep later and later. Didn't your doctor suggest you up the average age of your one-night stands to seventeen? Didn't you tell me he made that suggestion?"

There was a long pause before he replied: "Did you call to fight with me?"

"On the contrary, Tony. I need your help. I'm working on a very difficult investigation. Sam Tully and I. Are you game?"

"Of course, Swede."

Perhaps I would have discontinued the assault, fueled by that sudden loneliness and depression, if he had not lapsed into calling me Swede. Basillio thought all tall, blond women from Minnesota had to be of Scandinavian descent. Many are, but I'm not one of them. It re-infuriated me to hear him call me that.

"From your experience, Tony," I said icily, "is there a direct correlation between chronic infidelity and chronic foot pain?"

There was another long silence, then: "What's going on, Alice?"

"What do you think is going on?"

"Well, you don't sound so good."

"I'm not."

"What happened?"

I began to laugh at his question. What happened!

"You mean thirty years ago, Tony?"

"Look, Alice, you sound crazy. You sound like you don't like me right now. You sound childish. But Alice, I'm innocent. I'm in Los Angeles. This time my hands are clean."

"We've been together a long time, Tony. Longer than most marriages last."

"On and off."

"I don't like that phrase," I barked.

"You're the one who uses it all the time."

"I met someone, Tony."

"Oh? What's A.G. going to say about that?"

"And then he died."

"What!"

"You heard me. I met someone. But he died."

"Who was he?"

"His name was Alan."

"When did he die?"

"A few days ago."

"How long did you know him?"

"Not long."

"What happened to him?"

"He fell out of a building. Crashed through a window and smashed up on the sidewalk."

"I'm sorry. Did I know him?"

"No."

"In the business?"

"No."

"Something to do with this investigation you're involved in?"

"Yes."

"Had you slept with him?"

"No."

"Why not?"

I was laughing into the phone like a mad-woman. His last question — why not? — I found hilarious. And hilariously stupid. But I couldn't answer it.

"I'm going to have to hang up now, Tony."

"Wait!"

"What?"

"Any work?"

"I auditioned for a Parks Department spot. Voice-over."

"Look, I can get on a plane tonight. I could be in New York in the morning."

"What for?"

My sarcasm was laid on so heavily that he just let the receiver down onto the cradle without another word.

I felt like an idiot. And suddenly very hungry.

I rarely eat pasta in the summer, but I made myself a huge plate of very thin spa-ghetti topped with butter, garlic, and Par-mesan cheese.

Halfway through the debauch my agent called and informed me that I didn't get the voice-over job.

For some reason that made me feel better.

She told me she was exploring another possibility: a new TV cop show that was casting for an older female police lieutenant.

For some reason that made me feel worse.

I asked her nastily: "What happened to all your contacts with theatrical producers?" For good measure, I added, "You know, I was trained for the theater."

For dessert I had four fresh strawberries and half a banana.

Then Sam called. He bombarded me with questions: Did I have a bad hangover? Did I like barhopping with him? Did I have any further thoughts on my weird, inchoate (he actually used that word) hunches concerning no-cat Nope and Iron Betsy? Did I like his friend Turk Tolchin? Did I believe him? Did I think that Manny Soma was lying? Did I have any new thoughts on the dead kid (he meant Alan Petrie)? Did I have any idea what we should do next? Like put some new kinds of pressure on Ray Fields and Noelle Lightner?

I wasn't much help. I said to Sam: "Exhaustion is a factor."

"Ain't that the truth, honey. But one more time would be good. One more time around."

"Okay, Sam. I'll think."

"Yeah. You think and I'll think. Maybe you should take a long walk, honey. Clear your head. Do you know what I'm saying? Take one more bite of Montag."

When I hung up the phone, I was intrigued by what he had said . . . that last phrase . . . "one more bite of Montag."

I took a shower, put on some comfortable slacks and my walking sandals, tied my hair up, and took a walk.

It was a very odd walk, almost as if I had a gyroscope in my brainstem. I made no conscious choices of direction. I just seemed to be pointed this way or that.

I walked to Spring Street, then east, past Sam's building, and all the way to the Bowery.

It was almost five by then, and the day was cooling off.

All kinds of bits and pieces were jangling in my head — intellectual artifacts — Alan, Tony, Sam. Words. Things. Memories. Fantasies.

I turned north on the Bowery, right past Montag's loft. I stopped a few yards past it, turned, and looked at the building.

Was this what Sam wanted me to do?

Was this taking one more bite of Montag?

I walked to the curb and just stood there, staring up at the windows, the fire escape, the facade of the loft building.

Nothing came. I was looking at blank walls.

I thought of Mr. Wittgenstein.

About ten years ago I started going to different churches, looking for some kind of viable spiritual path. I got sidetracked into philosophy, and I became obsessed with Ludwig Wittgenstein. It was a short obsession, shorter than my fling with Buddhism or Catholicism or born-again fundamentalism.

What I still remember about all of that is Ludwig's dictum: "The limits of your language are the limits of your world."

And how do you know when you reach that limit?

It's easy. You'll know. It's like hitting a wall. *Whack.*

I moved on. I reached Houston Street and turned east.

I passed the entrance to Sara Delano Roosevelt Park, where I had met Hetta.

I kept walking all the way to the East River, where Ginger Petrie had been murdered.

Then I crossed Houston, to the north side of the street, and headed west again. It was finally beginning to get dark. Though I had already walked for almost two hours, I felt no fatigue at all. I felt as if I could walk a thousand miles.

At Crosby Street, I turned south and entered the Housing Works Café, a combination bookstore and coffee shop with the proceeds going for the most part to AIDS patients.

While I was not tired, I was thirsty. I ordered an iced tea and took a table in front of the children's bookshelf, which was next to the cooking shelf.

There was some tumult in the place — tables and chairs were being moved to prepare for a poetry reading.

I sipped my drink and watched the activity. Soon, I realized, they would want to move my table.

The tea was delicious. It had a bite.

I laughed. Sam again. Take another bite out of Montag.

Sitting there, it dawned on me that I could not remember clearly what Montag looked like.

That was bizarre. And it irritated me.

I took out my ballpoint pen, the fancy one, and tried to draw Montag's face on a napkin.

I got the slope of his head, that's all.

How pathetic I was. Why couldn't I reproduce his face?

What could I reproduce? What did I really know about Montag, other than that he was tortured and murdered in his loft with me unconscious on the floor?

It suddenly became very important that I reproduce in my head exactly what I knew.

I knew Montag was a liar. His cat was not walked in the park, as he said it was. Nor did the young woman who was supposed to walk the cat do so.

I knew Montag was a forger; Detective Lorenzo had told me so.

I knew Montag was a good and loyal friend and co-worker — so Ray Fields and Noelle Lightner had told me.

I knew Montag was the devil incarnate; Alan Petrie told me so.

I knew Montag had some kind of intense, unexplained relationship with a young woman named Ginger Petrie, who was murdered on the same night he was.

I knew that Montag created a guidebook that for a reason not yet determined used a cryptic symbol to mark some bars that no longer existed.

I knew Montag had an obsession with a long-dead New York City tavern keeper named Hiram Potter, and Potter's cat.

I knew Montag argued with a bartender who turned out to have once worked in a bar which was still listed in the current *New York by Night* but which had burned down three years ago.

I knew Montag could not have had anything real to do with either the murder or suicide of Alan Petrie — Montag was already dead. I knew that, but I didn't believe it.

I knew, although I had no evidence other than Alan's hatred, that his sister had been in love with Montag.

I knew that Montag had been a living contradiction and was now a dead one . . . because while he was a passionate historian of the New York tavern world, his guidebook was totally ahistorical. There was no Hiram Potter or Iron Betsy in *New York by Night*. The closest he came to talking about the past was the absurd listing of some vanished drinking establishments, none of which was more than three years gone.

I knew Montag had taken in a litter of orange tabby shorthairs with extra toes on their back feet — when Pia Jonas, because of her husband's illness, could no longer care for the cats.

And I knew, yes, I surely knew, that

Montag had a cat named Brat who could not be located.

Wasn't it funny that all my fragmentary lines of information about Montag ended up in one knot called Brat?

Always Brat.

From the beginning, the cat who was not there.

I had been so absorbed by my thoughts about Montag that I did not notice three impatient individuals try to move my table. One of them picked up my iced tea glass and rattled the ice cubes.

I walked home fast and called Sam the moment I got in.

"Okay, Sam," I said. "I took your advice."

"You mean you want to go out with me again tonight, Nestleton? You mean you want to hit some uptown bars?"

"No. I mean I took another bite at Montag."

He laughed. "You bite, I chew. Talk."

"Brat."

"Brat?"

"Yes. The cat. The cat we can't find. The cat Montag said was being walked in that park."

"But you already took care of this, honey. Didn't you find a lady in the park who told you what went down? And it got you no-where."

"I think I should go back, Sam. I think I should talk to her again. With you around. A new face with me."

"You think she was lying?"

"No."

"What else could she know? I mean, honey, if I remember correctly, the woman was not playing with fifty-two cards."

"Maybe we can get a little more out of her. Maybe something that would help us track down the fat lady with the funny hair. The one who took Brat from Ginger and brought him back the next day."

"If it was Brat."

"Well, there was a cat in the carrier. Hetta says she saw it. She says it was ugly, if I remember."

"How do you know you can find this Hetta again? That park does not rent benches by the month."

"Let's try."

"Okay. What the hell. You started off looking for Brat. It's always nice to end up where you started. Harry Bondo once told a guy — I think it was in the first book — 'Crazy killers go for triangles; smart killers work in circles.' "

"Tomorrow morning, Sam."

"Good enough. Ring my bell."

CHAPTER 14

I rang Sam's downstairs bell at nine-thirty the next morning. He was down fast, dressed with his usual crypto-derelict flair.

"I'm wearing a hat," he said, "because it may be a long day."

I replied: "It may be a very short day. Hetta may have nothing further to say. Maybe, like you suggested, she doesn't use that park anymore. Maybe she doesn't come to the park in the morning. Remember, I met her in the late afternoon."

"Then why are we here this early?"

"Because, Sam, she was feeding pigeons. I know that pigeons like to feed in the morning and afternoon. So, a compulsive pigeon feeder would make sure to time her feeding visits with the pigeons' needs, no matter how deranged said pigeon feeder was."

"Sometimes, Nestleton, you are one brilliant lady."

"Thank you."

"In fact, if a Harry Bondo series is ever resurrected, I will write you in as his sidekick."

"You are sweet."

"Of course, honey, I'll have to kill you off after two books."

"Understood."

We ate breakfast in a diner on Great Jones Street and Lafayette. I had an English muffin and coffee. Sam had an orange juice, one egg over a stack of pancakes, sausages, extra syrup, and coffee.

"I'm dieting," he explained. "No toast."

We entered the park at Houston and Forsythe. At this time of the morning, in summer, there were few people there.

Hetta was not at Rivington, where I had encountered her the first time. But at Hester Street I spotted her.

She was seated — no, sprawled — on a bench.

There were pigeons stalking back and forth around her, waiting for food, but she was not feeding them anything. Nor did she seem to have any bread available.

Her flamboyant mixture of clothes was the same, her heavy makeup the same, but there was something different about her behavior now.

She was talking and gesturing to herself, sometimes with agitation. I immediately thought: She was medicated the last time I saw her; now she isn't.

Now, in fact, there was no doubt that she

would have to deal with a homeless, indigent, perhaps recently released mental patient.

And this time she was surrounded by two battered valises and several shopping bags. In one of the bags I could see several pairs of broken sunglasses.

"You sure that's her?" Sam asked.

"Yes."

"Then we got trouble."

I did not bother to contradict him. We approached. She did not seem to acknowledge our presence.

"Hetta! Hetta!" I called out. She didn't respond.

"Don't you remember me?" I pressed, leaning very close to her face.

The woman started to talk even faster to herself. Nothing she said was comprehensible.

Sam motioned that I should step back. I did so.

He lit two cigarettes at the same time, then offered one to her. She grabbed it out of his hand like a mongoose attacking a snake and began to take huge, deep, sucking inhalations, babbling all the time.

She stared at Sam. Then she looked at me.

I smiled at her, trying to get her to remember me.

She kept smoking furiously, but her babbling changed to ugly curses directed at me.

She suddenly jumped off the bench, picked up one of her shopping bags, and flung it at me. It landed against my shoulder, the junk spilling all over the ground.

She started to scream. Her words were now, for the first time, comprehensible:

"Where is the girl? Where is the ugly cat? Where is the money? Where is the fat lady?"

Over and over again she repeated the questions, in no particular order, and while she was doing so, she kept reaching for me, trying to hurt me.

Sam kept me safe, continually blocking her path.

Finally Hetta took the burning stub of the cigarette, inverted it, and rammed it into her own cheek. She didn't scream. I did. Sam knocked the butt out of her hand.

Hetta slumped down on the bench.

"This is futile," Sam said.

We exited the park at the exact spot we had entered.

"I need another cup of coffee," Sam said.

He took me into an incredibly decrepit little joint on Houston Street, only a block from the park. The place described itself as the world's finest "knishery." The name

was Something Kimmel . . . no, not Kimmel
. . . Schimmel . . . Yonah Schimmel, perhaps. The sign was difficult to read.

To my astonishment, not only did Sam
have coffee but he also proceeded to de-
molish a huge kasha knish splattered with
mustard. I ordered tea but didn't touch it.

When he finished, he pushed the plate
away and said: "Sad, honey. Too sad for a
nice morning like this. Like they used to say
when you saw someone like Hetta — 'There
but for the grace of God go I.' "

I didn't respond.

"You okay, honey?"

"Of course."

"You don't like knishes?"

"Not really."

"They're nutritious. They're cheap.
They're diverse. They're happy."

How could a foodstuff be happy? Sometimes Sam misused the English language
with great daring.

He leaned over. "Are you sure you're
okay?"

"Yes."

"That madwoman could have hurt you."

"I'm aware of that."

"You're pale."

"It was the strangeness of it all, Sam."

"What's strange about a crazy acting out?"

"Not what she did. What she said."

"She was just talking out her head."

"No, she wasn't. Not at the end. Not when she started firing those questions at me. Do you remember the questions, Sam?"

"Yeah."

"Go ahead. Repeat them."

"Well, she said 'Where's the girl?' 'Where's the fat lady?' and 'Where's the cat?' "

"That's right."

"How is that strange?"

"It's obvious that Hetta remembered me. My presence then triggered her memory, what she had told me. The cat she asked about was Brat in his carrier. That's what she told me — that she had looked into the carrier and saw an ugly cat. The girl she mentioned is Ginger Petrie. That's the term she used for her when we talked — 'that girl.' And the fat lady is the one with the funny hair who always showed up, according to Hetta, took the carrier from the girl, and brought it back the next day."

"That makes sense. So what?"

"We're missing something."

"What?"

"There was another question, wasn't there? She kept yelling, 'Where's the money?' Now, listen to me, Sam. The last time I saw her, when she was rational, she never mentioned a thing about money."

"Got it."

"So, we have to believe that money was exchanged, that she had simply forgotten about it when she was medicated and fairly rational. But when she goes on automatic lunatic pilot, the whole truth comes out. She wants to know where the money is."

"Okay. So money was exchanged. But between who and who?"

"I don't know for sure. Maybe Ginger gave the fat lady money. Maybe the fat lady gave money to her. Maybe Ginger gave Hetta money — charity."

"What's the most logical scenario?" Sam asked.

"Logically? It has to be from Ginger to the fat lady."

"Why? For what?"

"For a service."

"What kind of service?"

"Maybe grooming or nail clipping," I speculated.

"Maybe."

"Or maybe just old-fashioned boarding. Maybe, Sam, it was the simplest of all transactions. Ginger takes the cat into the park. She delivers it to the fat lady. She pays her for a night's boarding. The next day the cat is returned."

"So you're saying this so-called fat lady is a cat-sitter . . . like you."

"Maybe. But cat-sitters don't usually work like that. I don't pick up cats. And I usually don't get paid up front. No, I think it is a boarding kennel."

"Those are expensive, honey. And there aren't any of them around here. Besides, why would Montag board his cat? It would be crazy. He hired you to sit for the cat."

"From what Hetta told me the first time I interviewed her, it seems the cat was boarded every other night."

"That is excessive."

"If it was a boarding kennel, Sam. But what about a plain old pet shop?"

"In the neighborhood?"

"Right. A pet shop with a small kennel in the back. They all have them."

"Agreed."

I reached into my purse and pulled out the now creased and worn Xerox of a generic orange tabby shorthair. I stared at it.

Sam said, "You forgot about vets. Many of them board cats too."

I folded the photo carefully and placed it in a convenient pocket.

"It could be a vet," I agreed, "but then

again, I don't think the cash would be passed if the fat lady was a veterinary assistant sent to pick up the cat."

Sam drained his cup. "So," he speculated, "we are about to canvass the neighborhood."

"I'm afraid we are."

"And we are looking for what? Pet stores?"

"Exactly. All pet stores in general. But specifically pet stores that have small kennel facilities."

"Cages, you mean?"

"Yes. And perhaps runs."

"Lead on," said Sam.

"No. *You* lead on, Sam. You know this neighborhood better than I."

"Okay. Off the top of my head I can think of four. One on Houston, just two blocks east of here. One on Avenue A. One on Avenue B. And a big one on Delancey."

We worked out a simple plan. We would enter each pet store together. I would ask about Brat, showing the Xerox of the breed photo. Sam would look for Brat on his own in the kennel area, if any. In other words, we would subtly separate after the entrance. This I believed was necessary. Who knew what was involved? Who knew if the pet store owner who had Brat would admit it?

The case was too murderous to expect any cooperation. Yes, the strategy made sense. It was a bit paranoid. Another term for it, one I prefer, would be cautionary.

Our first entrance, alas, into the Houston Street pet store, was flawed and delayed.

As I turned the knob of the door, I realized Sam was not beside me.

I stepped away from the door and spotted him gazing into the pet store window.

"Sam! Let's go!" I urged.

"Just a minute."

I walked over to see what had so quickly seduced him into abandoning the agreed-upon strategy.

He was staring at a huge glass tank in which were different kinds of tortoises.

"Take a look, honey. Did you ever see anything so beautiful?"

He was pointing at one medium-sized tortoise, a very dull speckled brown in color, whose rather monstrous face was peeking out from the shell.

"They're slow, ugly, a bit dim-witted, and very reflective. That's why they're beautiful, Nestleton. Do you get it? That's why I love tortoises."

"Let's go, Sam. We have a lot of stops to make."

"Sure, honey. But take a look at him."

"Are you certain it's a him?"

"You have a point. But what do you think Pickles would do if I brought a tortoise home?"

"I don't know."

"He couldn't hurt it, could he?"

"Probably not. But he could flip it over."

Sam stared dreamily at the thing.

"I have," I admitted, "absolutely no knowledge of the relationship between tortoises and cats."

"But there must be a place where they co-exist."

"Maybe in South America," I offered.

"Why there?"

"I don't know. It just seems possible to me that somewhere off the coast of Chile, on a rocky island, feral cats and tortoises are co-existing happily."

"Yeah, maybe you're right. Feral cats and big old tortoises make sense. Maybe the cats use the tortoises as taxis. They ride them up and down the beach."

Sam tapped out some kind of message to the tortoise on the window. Then we entered the shop together, as planned.

The proprietor was a very quiet-spoken Hispanic man. I showed him the cat picture and inquired if such a cat was currently being boarded in his establishment. While I questioned the man, Sam innocently perambulated the shop.

There was a section in the back with several kennel cages and a playpen, but there were only puppies in them, for sale.

The proprietor said he did not board cats and had never seen Brat.

Sam purchased a catnip mouse for Pickles, casually priced the tortoise in the window — it was $149.50 — and then we headed for the Avenue A store.

This place was primarily birds and fish. It had no boarding facilities at all.

The pet store on Avenue B, which we tried to visit next, was out of business.

The day was becoming very hot. We were walking much more slowly. Sam showed me a building on Avenue B where Charlie Parker had lived. There was a commemorative plaque on the building specifying that, because Parker had lived there, the building was now in the Landmarks Preservation Program.

Sam grew very wistful. "You like jazz, honey?"

"I can take it or leave it. I listen to music according to mood. And I'm in the mood to go now, Tully. We've got one more stop. That big store you mentioned on Delancey Street."

But he did not move. "Honey, I need a cold drink before I get dragged to Delancey."

So we went to one of those new café on Avenue B and Sam had a vodka and cranberry juice while I had some kind of nonalcoholic mango and apple mixture over crushed ice.

It was a pleasant place even though the other customers seemed to be children. I wondered to myself if Alan Petrie would have been comfortable there.

The Delancey Street pet store was, as they say, a completely different kettle of fish.

It was enormous and set up like one of those chain stores — Petco or Petland.

Two floors' worth of every kind of pet food for every kind of pet. The largest selection of cat litter in the Western world. Toys of all kinds, for dogs, cats, birds, ferrets, donkeys. Tanks and perches for tropical fish, tropical birds, geckoes, snakes, and centipedes.

The air conditioning was so heavy that the moment you walked in, you felt that someone had smacked you with an ice cube.

I grabbed the first employee I could find. She was very young and harried looking and wore a red blazer with the store's name stitched on the breast pocket.

She looked at the picture and smiled. She said the store did not board pets of any kind.

Well, that was that.

I waited for Sam to reappear. He might have gone downstairs, I thought.

The cat food section lured me in while I waited. I started walking up and down the aisles, studying the prices of the different bags of cat food — three pounds, ten pounds, fifty pounds.

For some reason, right then, I had a peculiar thought, almost a visual hallucination. I saw Crazy Hetta walking down these very aisles banging each cat food bag and cursing it and shouting: Where's the girl? Where's the fat lady? Where's the money? Where's the cat?

I suddenly barged into someone in the aisle.

"Excuse me," I said.

But it was only Sam.

"I have to show you something, honey."

He led me downstairs and all the way to the back.

"Take a look!" he exclaimed.

My God! It was a literal wall of kennel cages, piled high and wide, one next to another, one on top of another — and each one contained at least one cat.

I can't explain my sudden rush of excitement. Somehow I felt I had found what we were looking for . . . that we had stumbled upon something precious . . . the revelation . . . the scissor that would cut through all the knots.

"You check one side, Sam, and I'll check the other."

"For what?"

I exploded. "For what! Are you serious? For an orange tabby shorthair with peculiar toe formations on her back feet. Have you already forgotten why we're here?"

"Calm down, Nestleton. Take it nice and easy. These aren't boarded cats."

"What are they?"

"They're up for adoption. They're ASPCA cats. That's where they come from. This store is participating in a pet adoption program. Brat won't be here." He showed me the sign that explained the program.

The reality totally deflated me. I felt this last wild chase was now a three-hundred-pound Canada goose and it had landed right on me.

It didn't seem to bother Sam at all. He peered into cage after cage, saying he would like to take this one or that one back to Pickles . . . or that he could tell this one was mean or that one was psycho.

"I'm going home," I announced. "Suddenly I'm very tired."

"Are you kidding, Nestleton?" he shouted. "We just got started."

"You know any other pet stores around here?"

"No. But there's Chinatown. We're not far from there."

"Sam, you know as well as I that the pet stores in Chinatown don't board animals. They specialize in tropical fish and birds."

"True, true. But look. It's only a little out of the way, and I need some shrimp. Those big fat juicy shrimp at seven-ninety-five a pound, on Mott Street. So we compromise. A few pet store visits, and then my shrimp."

I was too depressed to argue, so my silence constituted agreement.

But when we passed a large pet store on Hester Street at Mott, with dozens of beautiful fish tanks in the window, Sam didn't even slow down.

I got very irritated. I mean, I knew he brought up the idea of inquiring about Brat in a few Chinese pet stores as a ruse to get me to accompany him on his shrimp-buying expedition. But a bargain is a bargain, no matter how imprecisely it is stated.

I stopped in my tracks.

"What?" he asked innocently.

I pointed to the pet store entrance.

"They don't sell shrimp," he said. "At least not by the pound."

I didn't smile. I was moving from irritation to anger. Sam picked up on the mood change and made a gesture of surrender.

We entered the store.

From behind the cash register, two snarling hounds of hell — Rottweilers — launched themselves at us.

I fell back against the door.

Sam caught me with one arm and with the other flailed out at the attacking creatures, trying to ward off their drooling jaws.

Then I heard a loud noise. It sounded like a grunt, an explosive grunt.

It was actually a command.

The dogs dropped down instantly, as if they had been shot. They lay still except for their excited panting.

A Chinese woman had suddenly materialized just a few feet from us.

"I am very sorry," she said.

Sam whispered in my ear: "You happy now, Nestleton? Can we get out of here and get that damn shrimp?"

But I wasn't ready to leave.

The short woman standing in front of me in traditional garb and flanked by her repentant beasts was quite stout.

In fact, she was out-and-out fat.

And her hair was done in a strange variation on the bowl cut.

There was no doubt about it. I was looking at someone who could be, in Hetta's words, a fat lady with funny hair.

I pulled the breed photo out of my pocket and held it up.

She stared at the image.

"Brat," I said simply. "I am looking for this cat. His name is Brat."

She grabbed the paper from my hand, crumpled it, and flung it down to the floor.

Then she began to chastise me with fury. "Why are you late? Where is the money? Believe me, I will get rid of those cats if I am not paid today. I went to the park. I kept going there. I saw no one. Where is my money? And what has happened to the girl I always deal with? What is going on?"

I was so astonished by her outburst that I couldn't speak.

"How many cats are you boarding?" Sam asked.

The woman headed toward the back of the store, gesturing angrily that we should follow.

She led us deep into the store, past the glittering tanks filled with the most beautiful fish I had ever seen. Even the carp were resplendent.

Then we saw the large, spotlessly clean kennel cages.

Five of them.

Brat was in one.

And in the next one. And the next.

They were all Brat.

Five orange tabby shorthairs, caged singly.

Was I looking at Bright's litter? Was I looking at the five surviving members of the original litter, which numbered seven?

The woman barked, "The monthly payment was due five days ago."

I opened each of the five cages and carefully, gently, stroked the cat inside, feeling its back feet.

Yes! Each had at least one extra toe on at least one of his or her back feet.

The woman was getting angrier and angrier.

"I went out of my way for that girl! She wanted to rotate the cats. So I would pick one up and bring her another the next day. But I don't like to be made a fool of. You pay me now or I'll take them all to the ASPCA."

"Miss," I said gently, "I don't think any further boarding payments will be made.

We'll take care of the cats. We'll take them out of here."

"How are we going to do that?" Sam murmured. "You really going to take them home? All five of them?"

"No," I said. "We'll call Pia Jonas. She'll be so happy to hear most of the litter is alive and well and together, she'll take them all."

"Wishful thinking," he said.

Sam was wrong. I phoned Pia Jonas from the pet store. After the initial shock and disbelief, she sounded like a delirious schoolchild who has been given the Christmas gift of her dreams. She said she would come right over as fast as she could — but she no longer had cat carriers to transport the beasts.

While still on the phone I noticed that the store sold several kinds of those new fabric-and-leather carriers — soft-sided ones.

"Just get here," I told Pia. "Sam and I will take care of the transportation."

After the phone call, I negotiated with the woman on the price of four carriers. A large one that would accommodate two cats, and three small ones.

I paid with my last remaining credit card, and Sam and I began to transfer the five Brats to their carriers. The animals' mellowness dissipated somewhat during the transfer; one began to screech as if being tortured, and one bit Sam's nose.

When our job was complete, the fat woman went about her business, and Tully and I sat down wearily on some large, empty cartons.

The two Rottweilers were still eyeing us. They sat together about two feet away. They made me nervous, but there was nothing I could do. We were all sitting and waiting.

I noticed the expression on Sam's face.

"What's so funny?"

"Nothing."

"Then why are you grinning like that?"

"I was just thinking about how pathetic anticlimaxes are."

"I'm not following you."

"Well, look, honey. Let's face it, you thought from the beginning that all you really had to do was find Montag's cat and poof! All would be revealed. Even I began to believe it. So look what happened. We found not one but five Brats. And we still don't know a damn thing."

I couldn't argue with that. I knew he was right. It was over.

"Let's just get the cats safely back to Pia Jonas and we can retire," I said wearily.

"Amen, honey."

About ten minutes later we heard the front door of the pet shop open.

"Your friend is here," the proprietor called.

Sam and I stood up and began to gather the carriers.

"I'll take the double one, Sam. You grab two singles and Pia will take the other one. Okay?"

"Sure."

Suddenly we heard the Chinese woman call out again, in a louder voice: "Wait!"

I looked up. Pia was heading toward us very quickly.

Then I realized it wasn't Pia Jonas. It was a tall, thin man in a loose raincoat and he had a stick in his hand.

I saw the stick emit sparks before I heard the deafening roar.

Sam pulled me down.

The figure kept firing his pump-action shotgun at the cages until they and the wall behind them were in smithereens.

The man was reloading.

That was when the Rottweilers struck. The dogs got him by the neck and thigh and sent him hurtling to the floor, screaming as he landed only inches from me.

Then everything was quiet except for the dogs' hard panting.

I lay on the floor shaking with fear, my nostrils filled with the stench of gunpowder and blood.

The shooter was unconscious. The dog bites in his neck were bleeding profusely.

I saw Sam crawling toward me.

"You alive?"

"Yes."

"He was going for those cats, honey. He didn't know they were out of the cages."

Sam took out his handkerchief and pressed it against the man's neck, trying to stanch the bleeding.

Sam grinned, sardonically this time. "I guess Pia Jonas changed her mind about taking those cats."

I tried to get up, but I was too weak.

I could hear the Asian woman on the phone talking to a 911 operator.

"Would you believe it?" Sam asked.

He was standing over the shooter, staring directly into the man's face. Sam seemed about to lose his footing. He was swaying slightly.

"What's the matter, Sam? Do you know him?"

"I think I do. I think we finally made contact with that bartender. Ted Lary."

CHAPTER 15

The next forty-eight hours were hellish.

After the police and EMS people allowed us to depart, we realized that the family of toe-challenged tabbies had no home at all anymore.

So we took them all to my loft in a cab.

You can imagine Bushy's and Pancho's response as we deposited the five cats in four carriers onto the floor.

My cats went bananas.

Bushy began acting like Pancho, flinging himself around the apartment with abandon.

Old Pancho began to act even stranger. He successively climbed up and sat on the top of each carrier, glaring down on the imprisoned orange tabby.

We quickly moved those carriers out of the apartment and into the hallway. Since I was on the top floor, the cats could go up no further. We prevented them from escaping down the stairs by barricading the staircase with boxes. They were going to be a nuisance to remove every time I wanted to take the stairs, but what could I do?

We put out food and water bowls and a

litter box and then freed the kitties from their cells so that they might inspect their new, temporary home. There were already several frayed runners and mats in the hall.

The five Brats seemed to have been totally unaffected by the shotgun attack.

Sam and I were not so resilient. When he left my place to go home, he was walking like a zombie and muttering to himself — Why the hell were all the cats there? Why would anyone want to kill them?

As for me, it was the smell I couldn't extinguish — the gunpowder and the blood from the dog bites.

The next morning when I got up, I was moving slowly and stiffly — not zombielike, the way Sam had moved, but rather as though I had arthritis in all my joints, without, thankfully, the accompanying pain.

Detective Lorenzo phoned at noon.

"How are you doing, Miss Nestleton?" he asked. He had arrived at the embattled pet store three hours after the attack. I told him why I was there and I told him about Pia Jonas's obvious orchestration of the assault — how I had called her to pick up Montag's cats, which had once been hers, how she never showed but sent a madman instead.

"Fine," I lied. "I'm just fine."

"We cannot locate Miss Jonas. We issued a warrant for her arrest. We also found a bank deposit slip on Lary. The bank informed us he had deposited a $5,500 check made out to him from one Manuel Soma. Do you know that name, Miss Nestleton?"

"Ask Ted Lary, Detective. You found it in his wallet."

"Ted Lary is dead. He died an hour ago. A massive coronary. Probably induced by shock and arterial bleeding. So I am asking you again — who is this Soma?"

"Lary's boss at Habana Blue. A bar he once worked. Uptown, I believe. Soma now runs a restaurant in Abingdon Square. It's called Nope."

"Well, we'll want to have a word with him. I mean — what was the money for? If Lary was crazy enough to take out a pet shop in Chinatown, he was crazy enough to take out Montag on the Bowery."

I was silent.

"Are you there, Miss Nestleton?"

"Yes."

"Tell me again, would you — was Ted Lary there to kill you or those cats? Or both?"

"I don't know."

"You've been conducting a parallel investigation, haven't you?"

"I was. No more."

"Did you, while conducting this parallel investigation, ever get a whiff of motive?"

"No."

"Can you speculate on a motive?"

"No."

"All right. Just one more thing. While Lary was moving in and out of consciousness before he died, he was talking a lot, shouting out incoherent phrases and names. One of the words he kept repeating was a woman's name. Betsy. It sounded like Iron Betsy. Maybe that first word is some kind of nickname. He could have even been saying *ironic* Betsy. We couldn't make it out. At any rate, Miss Nestleton, do you know anybody named Iron Betsy?"

"It sounds like a laundry detergent," I noted.

"Not funny," said Lorenzo. He was right. But it was futile to bare my soul to this detective. Nothing made sense to me, and nothing I could tell him about Iron Betsy would make sense to him. Besides, I had learned early on that Detective Lorenzo did not believe in my rendition of the most basic elements of the drama — like why I was at Montag's that evening.

It dawned on me that we had all been cursed . . . Like the old Yiddish curse someone had once told me about. It goes something like this: "May you live in a beautiful house with fifty magnificent bedrooms. And may you spend each night roaming from room to room, bed to bed, unable to sleep."

I knew all about the terrible curse of sleeplessness.

Montag, however, went one better. His curse was to make all the participants and their acts *motiveless.*

Lorenzo hung up before I could illuminate our shared legacy.

His last words were: "We'll pick up this Jonas and Soma sooner or later. Believe me, we'll get them."

I went out into the hallway, shutting the door quickly so that Pancho and Bushy would not escape, and insinuated myself among the toe-challenged brood. Two of them had of their own accord crawled back into their carriers to snooze. One was trying to claw down the boxes barricading the stairs. The other two sat side by side, occasionally grooming themselves, casting furtive, inquiring glances at me.

Soon I fell fast asleep right there in the hallway, on a tattered mat.

When I awoke from my nap it was late

afternoon, and the five tabbies now considered me one of the litter. They climbed on me, rubbed against me, stuck their little noses into my face, and expected me to sing with them.

What, I thought, am I doing on a mat in my own hallway? It was ridiculous.

I went back inside the apartment and consoled Bushy and Pancho.

I had no idea how I would resolve the feline domicile problem, but I did know that before I could figure out what to do with them, I would have to marshal my resources.

Sitting down at the dining room table with a pad and ballpoint pen, I proceeded to estimate what kind of food and cat litter I would require, and in what quantity.

As I was figuring, from time to time I walked to the door and peered out the peephole at the clan.

It occurred to me that I was becoming fond of them. They were endearing. They seemed to have a goofy normality in spite of the fact that each of them had been an assassination target and each of them had at least one peculiar toe formation on each back foot.

They were also noisy; I like noisy cats.

And they were all, except for one of the females, a bit plump.

Their orange coats were dull, yes, but that was to be expected given that they had been living in cages.

They were remarkably similar in size and conformation — a very consistent litter.

The easiest way to tell them apart was by their whiskers — a wild mix of colors and lengths.

I continued my computations. It appeared to me that with careful shopping, a hundred dollars would buy enough litter and dry and canned food for the next thirty days. I had no idea of their food habits. If they were as picky as Bushy and Pancho, I would be in trouble.

My computations had made me hungry. Or so I believed. The fact was, there was every reason for me to be hungry. I had eaten nothing since the morning of our pet shop journey.

I made myself a large, crude BLT on stale white bread. It was scrumptious. I was wolfing it down when the phone rang.

I was sure it was Lorenzo again, with more questions that I either couldn't or wouldn't answer. So I let the answering machine deal with the call.

The voice that left the message was very weak. It wasn't Lorenzo. It was more familiar.

Then the voice got louder, and I heard a desperate plea: "I need help. I need help."

God! It was Sam. And he was obviously in terrible trouble. I grabbed the receiver.

"Sam! What's the matter?"

His voice had gotten low again. "I got pain, honey. Up and down my body. I can't move."

"You've got to get to the hospital. Now."

"I tell you, honey, I *can't*. I can't move. Help me, Nestleton."

"Where are you, Sam?"

"At the Oasis."

"On Orchard Street?"

"Yeah. I . . ." His voice trailed off in pain.

I yelled into the phone: "I'll be there. I'm coming, Sam."

I slammed the receiver down and raced downstairs through the frightened brood.

I cursed Sam as I flailed about on the street for a cab. It figured that Sam would fall ill in a bar — he lived in them. But to get sick in an ugly place like the Oasis was too much to bear.

I got a cab. I was at the Oasis in ten minutes. Sam was sprawled, half alive, in a back booth.

How he had gotten to a phone to call me, I couldn't even imagine.

I sat down beside him and slid his arm

around my neck. "I'll get you to the hospital. Don't worry."

He looked up at me sadly. "I'm sorry, honey," he said. "I had no choice."

And he said it as if he was no longer mortally ill.

Then a figure moved close to our table and sat down right across from us. It was a woman with a cotton shawl around her head. She had a book in her hand, inverted, and jutting out from the pages was the barrel of a pistol. The title of the book, for what it's worth, was *Diary of a Country Priest*, by Bernanos. A Frenchman.

I was so frightened and confused that it took me a full minute to understand that the woman with the gun was Pia Jonas. And to realize further that poor Sam had been forced, under extreme duress, to fetch me here.

Pia spoke to me: "This is not going to take long. First I am going to tell you a story. Then I am going to ask you to do something. If you listen carefully . . . if you do what I ask . . . then you will be able to save your friend's life. And your own."

The woman looked exhausted. But the hand that held the ugly semiautomatic was as steady as a rock.

"I did not lie to you about my relationship

185

with Louis Montag. I did lie about when I last saw him. It was only a few weeks ago. He called out of the blue and begged me to meet him. I went. He presented me with several gifts, including a beautiful bracelet and earrings. It was all very strange, like I was a soldier and he was giving me medals. I asked him what this was all about. He told me he could no longer hide his triumph; that I had made his triumph possible; that he must share his joy with me. I had no idea what he was talking about.

"The man is truly mad, I thought. But I did listen to him. He told me that years ago his research had uncovered the secret of Hiram Potter's cat — Iron Betsy. Her ferocious reputation came from the fact that, in whatever dwelling she lived, there was always a fire that destroyed everything. That's right, he said, wherever she lived, the building unfailingly burned down. And her reported physical deformity was six toes on the back feet.

"I asked him where he had obtained that information. He said it didn't matter. He got crazier. He told me he had taken my litter when my husband got sick not because he was a good Samaritan, not because we were lovers and he wanted to ease my burden, but because he realized my litter of six-toed cats were the direct descendants of Iron Betsy.

"I laughed at his claim, of course. It was ridiculous. Louis was hurt. He said I shouldn't scoff because he had done the impossible. He had recreated the New York City bar scene of 1780. I had no idea what he was talking about. He then took me to Hell's Kitchen. There was a burned-out storefront on Eleventh Avenue. He said it used to be a bar called Agatha's. Three months ago his assistant, Ginger Petrie, had started working there as a waitress. She had replaced the existing bar cat with one of Bright's litter. Sure enough, an electrical fire then destroyed the place."

I looked at Sam, who raised his eyebrows. No bar called Agatha's had received one of those strange notations in *New York by Night*. But then again, it probably would have, in the next edition — if Montag had lived.

Our captor was angered by my glances at Sam, by my interruption of her story. She leaned across the table and pressed the barrel of her weapon into my cheek.

"Listen to me! I told you to listen."

I nodded in petrified assent and apology. The barrel was very cold.

Pia Jonas resumed: "Right there on the

street, in front of what had once been a bar, he started to dance and laugh. I was appalled. He said he had recreated a three-hundred-year-old curse — a cat with the power to destroy, to burn, to triumph. Over what? I wondered. I said I didn't believe him. He showed me the latest edition of his guidebook. He pointed out several bars listed with a symbol next to the name — an N in parentheses. He said all of them had been visited by Ginger and one of the Bright litter. And all those places are gone now.

"He took me home in a cab. He said as he left that he was eternally grateful to me and that I should remember him with love, as he did me.

"The next few days I didn't know what to do. Was Louis completely insane? Or was he an arsonist? I decided to check up on the bars he had mentioned. I found in one sense he was telling me the truth. Every one of them had burned down. But the one where lives were lost was called Habana Blue — three dead.

"If Louis was really setting all those fires, he had to be stopped. I went to the police, to the arson squad, to report what I knew. They told me there had been no sign of arson in the Habana Blue fire. They said they needed evidence. I could give them none.

"I used to work in the City Clerk's office so I knew how to locate licenses of any kind. I tracked down the owner of Habana Blue and told him what Montag told me. Mr. Soma remembered Ginger Petrie and the orange tabby bar cat. He had lost a brother in the fire."

I felt Sam prodding me surreptitiously. I knew what he was signaling: that it was now a whole lot clearer why Manny Soma had no bar cat at his new place — fear.

Pia Jonas started to speak more quickly, as if she were being pursued, which of course she was.

"Soma took me to see a former Habana Blue bartender who had lost a niece and a nephew in the fire. Ted Lary was now working at a bar on Fourteenth Street called Bass Line. I repeated my story to him.

"After he heard what I had to say, he called Montag and demanded that Louis come over to the bar. Louis arrived. Soma and I hid in the back of the place. We heard Lary accuse him of setting the fire at Habana Blue. Louis denied everything. There was a tremendous argument. Then Louis refused to talk anymore. He didn't leave the bar, though. He remained there and started a conversation with a stranger — the man sitting beside you now."

She laid her head down on the table. The gun still did not waver.

I understood now why Montag had sought a cat-sitter. He must have intuited that Ted Lary was dangerous. A cat-sitter in his apartment would be insurance against an unwitnessed attack. Or so he thought.

Pia Jonas went on.

"After Louis left the Bass Line, we agreed that he must be stopped. Louis Montag and Ginger were murderers. Ted Lary and Manny Soma did not believe the cats were demons from hell with magical powers to start fires. But they did decide that the cats were part of the killing and the burning. I loved those cats, but I had to agree with them. Soma and Lary did not discuss their plans with me, not the specifics anyway. They didn't want me implicated. They were grateful for my information. I went home.

"I know they killed Louis Montag and Ginger Petrie. They beat Louis before they killed him, but he never revealed the whereabouts of the cats.

"When you called me from that pet shop and told me you had found Bright's litter, I called Ted Lary immediately. He went to do . . . what he felt had to be done."

She sat up suddenly, very straight in the booth.

"So that is the story," she said. "There is nothing more I can tell you. Was Louis a murderous psychotic who loved to torch places? Was he a deranged scholar who thought he had found a piece of New York City history so precious he had to master it and recreate it? If one of my tabbies became the bar cat in this place where we're sitting right now, do you think it would burn down? Do you think Louis believed that every one of Bright's litter is a cursed cat with the magic of fire in its blood? Did Ginger Petrie believe that? Why did she become Louis's helpmate in such a horrible scheme? For love? For money?

"I don't know the answers. But I do know this. Those cats have to die. They have to be destroyed. I love them dearly, but somehow all those deaths are on their heads. And on mine. I bred them. Whether all the hocus-pocus is true or not, Iron Betsy's line must end now!"

She waited.

"I don't understand what you're saying," I told her.

"Kill them, Alice Nestleton! Every one of them. Now. Bring me evidence they are dead, and I will not kill your friend here."

"I don't understand what you are saying," I repeated.

"I am saying that because we don't know how those places caught fire . . . because we don't know if my six-toed tabbies are devils from some long-lost time . . . they must all die."

"Then I will take you to them," I offered.

"No! I can't do it. You do it. How you do it, I don't care. But you must kill them."

She placed a wristwatch on the table, a very thin, old-style lady's watch.

"You have a hundred and twenty minutes," she noted, pointing the gun barrel at Sam. "Two hours." She added, unnecessarily, "Or he dies."

I slipped unsteadily out of the booth. For one brief moment, as I was walking out of the bar, I thought, *Call Lorenzo. You must tell the police.* But the resoluteness of the woman stopped me. I had the distinct feeling that she would kill Sam before she was taken down by the police.

The horror of the situation nauseated me. What did she want as proof? Their heads? Their ears? I looked for a cab.

How simple it all seemed now. A psychotic guidebook author projecting fanciful tales about an ancient bar cat onto a few innocent kittens whose only resemblance to Iron Betsy was probably one extra toe.

But why was there no evidence of arson in any of the fires?

Was Pia right — if arson could not be proved, the cats must die? Nothing else mattered. Sooner or later coincidence becomes inevitability. Ginger Petrie appears in a bar. The bar cat vanishes. Ginger introduces an orange tabby with six toes into the bar. The place goes up in flames. Ginger and the cat survive.

Did the cat smoke in bed?

One time is a coincidence. Twice, a rare coincidence. Three times and more — and no sign of arson — is gospel.

I found myself weaving and reeling on the sidewalk.

Was I to become an executioner? For Sam's sake? For the city's sake? Did I have a choice?

One hour and forty minutes later, I returned to the Oasis, lugging a carrier.

Sam's grizzled old head was back on the table. He seemed to be sleeping. Two empty glasses were in front of him; at least his captor had bought him some drinks.

Pia Jonas was still sitting straight, her watch on the table.

Her gun was still obscured by the book, but now that was against her chest, as if she were holding a child. For the first time I could see her fingers on the trigger.

I lifted the carrier to the top of the table.

Tears came to her eyes.

One of her hands moved to the clasp. Then she hesitated.

"I want to thank you," she whispered. "I want to thank you from the bottom of my heart. I did not have the strength to do this."

Her face contorted as she opened the carrier, saying over and over again, "I have to be sure . . . I have to be sure."

Then she screamed — and fired — as twenty-five pounds of infuriated Maine coon cat burst out of the bag and landed on her head before leaping to the top of the booth behind her.

Bushy does not like to be put in a carrier. He screeches for a while and then goes silent, plotting his revenge on the person who will open it, the same person, he assumes, who put him in it.

Pia Jonas was knocked halfway under the table. The pistol fell to the floor and slid five feet away from her. The two shots she fired had splintered the wood behind Sam's head.

Patrons began to shout.

Neither Sam nor I made any effort to

impede Pia Jonas's movement as she fled the bar.

Three hours later, I reached Detective Lorenzo and reported to him the incident at the Oasis and the story Pia Jonas had told us.

He immediately issued warrants for Soma — the charge, murder — and Jonas — the charge, conspiracy and assault with a deadly weapon. Of course they were already being sought.

Bushy was given a medal for valor, which he ate with relish.

Soma was arrested six days later in Watertown, New York. He was released shortly thereafter because my secondhand testimony, and Sam's, were insufficient to indict him on a murder one charge.

Lorenzo, however, was optimistic. He told me, "When we get the Jonas woman, we'll put Soma away."

During that conversation I asked him about the investigation into the death of Alan Petrie.

"We're looking at a number of scenarios. But remember," he said, "I'm not working that case."

"What scenarios?" I asked bitterly.

He picked up on my mood; he didn't want

to alienate me now. I think Lorenzo believed that Pia Jonas would contact me again. And so he was more or less honest with me.

"I don't believe Lary or Soma had anything to do with it. In fact, more and more we're leaning to suicide."

"But you people must have had some kind of evidence that prevented you from accepting it as suicide from the beginning."

"Not positive evidence. Negative evidence," he declared cryptically.

"And what kind of animal would that be?"

"Well, the kid had a pair of binoculars at the spot where he jumped. People who are about to kill themselves by jumping out a window do not usually look through binoculars before they jump."

It was too depressing to continue. It was too nineteenth century. Young men don't die for older women anymore. And no one should die for me, ever . . . except on stage.

And to be honest, I would never believe it. Yes, Alan had jumped. He was not pushed. I believed that. But the cancer in his heart was not a forty-one-year-old actress/cat-sitter.

As for the five Brats? They met a most wonderful fate, thanks to Sam Tully.

Since I could not keep them in the hallway, I started making calls and offering them for adoption. There were no takers. Then Sam advised me, "Nestleton, I don't like to interfere, but you are going about this the wrong way. You gotta play to their strength."

"What strength?"

"Think show biz, honey. Demon seed. Six toes. Play it up."

He created a single poster for me to place in the bodega on Hudson Street. It read in flame-red Magic Marker:

Six-toed Demon Cats for Adoption
FIVE BEAUTIFULLY EVIL CATS
AVAILABLE. Orange tabby shorthairs. Six toes on back feet. Believed to be ancestors of the infamous Colonial cat, Iron Betsy.

No Bars or Restaurants Considered. Cats Allergic to Alcohol.

I put the notice up the next day. All five cats were adopted within twenty-four hours. All went to excellent homes. Two of them to a beachfront mansion in Southampton. One to a young couple with two small children in Tribeca. One to a French cultural attaché. And the last one, the thin female, to a wholesaler in the meat market. What a time she'll have.

My phone is still ringing from that single notice in one shop.

And that is how I spent my summer vacation.

The employees of Thorndike Press hope you have enjoyed this Large Print book. All our Thorndike and Wheeler Large Print titles are designed for easy reading, and all our books are made to last. Other Thorndike Press Large Print books are available at your library, through selected bookstores, or directly from us.

For information about titles, please call:

(800) 223-1244

or visit our Web site at:

www.gale.com/thorndike
www.gale.com/wheeler

To share your comments, please write:

Publisher
Thorndike Press
295 Kennedy Memorial Drive
Waterville, ME 04901